BOUND IN THE DARK
Dark Sons
Book 6

ANN JENSEN

Published by Blushing Books
An Imprint of
ABCD Graphics and Design, Inc.
A Virginia Corporation
977 Seminole Trail #233
Charlottesville, VA 22901

Ann Jensen
Bound in the Dark

eBook ISBN: 978-1-63954-387-8
Print ISBN: 978-1-63954-388-5

Cover Art by ABCD Graphics & Design

Chapter 1

If you never ask yourself 'What have I gotten myself into'
then you aren't truly living your life.

T*wo months ago*

An undercurrent of sensual delight and primal need washed
through Diana as she stepped inside Dark Secrets. Only here
could she shed the exacting demands of her everyday life and
exist inside the moment. The siren call of temptation was
something she didn't usually indulge. But lately she longed to
forget, to lose herself in the pleasure this place promised.

Clubs, even those that catered to the darker desires of
human nature weren't unknown to Diana. Hell, there had
been plenty of times visiting one was a necessary part of her
job. But for some reason, this one was special.

While doing a job as a favor for her sister, Diana had discovered the private BDSM club. The place had intrigued her so much she had obtained a membership even if it hadn't been exactly necessary. Seeing first hand what her targets had been doing inside had been her flimsy excuse.

After a single night of watching the members' hedonistic activities, it had become an obsession. Her dreams filled with the idea of exploring the fantasies the club offered. Months of observing had done nothing but build the hunger inside her. Diana couldn't resist the urge any longer to be more than a bystander.

Her whole life had been rigidly laid out, spent in the service of others. Control was critical to survival. Careful and precise with everything. Each breath, every movement, even the words she spoke, were influenced by her brutal childhood training.

Breaking free of their control years ago had almost cost her her life. The training she had endured wasn't as easy to shake. Even now, forgetting those lessons might cost her her life, but she longed for just a few moments of mental relaxation.

Perhaps participating in a scene wasn't the best way to break the conditioning that kept her wound so tight. But nothing else Diana had tried in her twenty-nine years had worked. Studies said that giving up control willingly was a freeing experience. And she had chosen the one man she was willing to give it to.

Master H.

The members of Dark Secrets hid their identities behind club names making her research into who to trust complicated, but not impossible. Her current identity, Luna Hunt, had been expensive to obtain but necessary in order to pass their government level background checks. The cyber security of the club was above her meager hacking skills so she had been forced to use other talents to identify the regulars.

Hell, if she was the type of woman who trusted easily she could have accepted one of the many offers to scene a long time ago. But her mind didn't work like that. Diana needed to know everything about a person. Her obsessive planning was the only reason she was still alive.

The man she had chosen wasn't the logical choice. He wasn't the safest or even the least likely to endanger her cover. But Highdive had fascinated her from the moment she'd seen him through her sniper scope. And now no one else would do.

The man was a fascinating example of everything she shouldn't want in a man. Enforcer for his Motorcycle Club the Dark Sons, he should be someone she avoided. But she couldn't stay away.

Years in the Marines had crafted his body into a solid wall of muscle. Like her, he trained everyday. But it wasn't the perfectly sculpted muscles or his deadly skills that attracted her. It was his eyes.

A fascinating shade of green that changed with his mood. It was obvious when looking into them that he could take on any challenge. He wouldn't give up until he mastered whatever he needed to succeed. They showed his complete focus on whatever task he was assigned.

Diana's dreams had been filled with fantasies of those eyes focused completely on her. In them he wouldn't give up until he succeeded where so many lovers before him had failed.

At Dark Secrets he was known as Master H. An expert in Shibari. Every time he used his rope to turn a sub into a living piece of artwork Diana had been entranced. A shiver ran across her skin, she wanted the intense concentration when he bound a woman and strung her up on display focused on her. He drew the inner core that was the essence of submission from every sub he played with.

The idiots around here described him as a cold heartless machine. They feared his indifference as much as they respected him. Diana understood what they didn't. Emotions got in the way of control. He focused on creating perfection. So there was no room for messy feelings.

Having a scene with him was considered both an honor and a curse. Master H played a woman's body like a savant but rarely spoke to his partners once aftercare was complete. Rumor was that many hearts had been broken against the stone wall that was his indifference.

Most women craved an emotional connection. But not Diana. She respected the cool way he interacted with women. How he made sure they didn't misunderstand his intentions.

It didn't even appear to be the sex that Highdive enjoyed, though he did obtain release, but rather the perfecting of his art. He would play with a sub several times but once he figured out how to shatter her with pleasure he rarely chose her again.

He was perfect for her. Diana's life was complicated and she couldn't afford emotional entanglements. The truth was she had nothing to offer a partner except her body and that only on a limited time frame.

Only inside the club's walls could she indulge. It was a calculated risk, but she would allow herself the freedom to give over control in this one place with this one man. A few times with Master H would have to be enough to satisfy her new cravings.

Diana smoothed down the silk robe she had chosen for the night to settle her nerves. Her plan was set. She had prepared for every possible response. She'd even tightly braided her long dark hair away from her face in the way she had noticed he preferred.

The folder in her hand was cool. She focused on not gripping it too tightly. The stiff manilla paper contained her limits list, medical information, and club profile. Master H always requested printed copies of those items from the club receptionist before he played with someone new and she hoped to save him the time. Another sign that she was prepared.

Her body hummed with anticipation. Highdive sat relaxed, talking with two men from his motorcycle club in a back booth. Sweat dropped down her back as she mentally prepared to approach him. Why was she so nervous?

Her sexual interactions in the past had been at best mediocre. Initiated more out of curiosity or if she had alternative goals in mind other than pleasure. The worst-case he would reject her. Or not live up to expectations.

That was what she really feared. Ever since she had noticed him, her body had come alive with a need she struggled to contain. Hopefully, giving in would help her regain focus. Even if he turned her down it would be better than all the what-ifs that plagued her mind.

It was ten o'clock. If he had been waiting for someone they would have already been there. She needed to approach him or he would soon search out one of his regular playmates. She slipped out of her shoes and robe, and folded it neatly into one of the many cubbies along the wall.

She wasn't body shy, but walking across the club naked for the first time, without shaking, took all of her self control. There were plenty of other naked people as well as others in outfits that didn't cover anything important. She had considered wearing something designed for temptation but thought it was a waste of time. Naked was more honest and she hoped Master H would agree.

When she reached the area where he sat, she stopped just outside conversational distance and dropped to her knees. Diana had practiced the motion hundreds of times to make sure she didn't embarrass herself. She placed the folder on the floor in front of her knees then settled her hands onto her thighs with her eyes downcast to wait.

The men's low voices were a rumble against her skin. Her excitement grew as they finished talking. She could feel their gazes and barely resisted the urge to look up.

"Who are you here for, darlin'?" a smooth Texan voice, that she recognized as Ink, asked. He and his partner Hannibal were well known at the club for wild chaotic scenes that didn't appeal to her.

"Sir, I am available if Master H is interested."

"Shame." Ink chuckled.

She kept her head bowed. From between her lashes she saw the two men stand. Ink scooped her folder off the ground and she heard the slap of it hitting the table. They left her kneeling in front of the table where Master H sat and headed out onto the floor. Nerves caused her stomach to clench, but she breathed through her nose and forced her body to remain relaxed.

The hard floor wasn't exactly comfortable as minutes slid by. The urge to scan the room for danger was like an itch under her skin. In all of her imagining of this moment she hadn't accounted for how she would feel sitting there not knowing if he was reading over her information. Not being able to read his face was nerve-wracking.

There was little she could do to affect the outcome at this point. Her path was chosen no matter where it ended. A sense of peace washed through her as she accepted that. Tonight was about giving over control. Right or wrong she would live with that choice and its consequences.

"Look at me." Master H's voice was deep and smooth.

She looked up and her breath caught. His green eyes glowed in the dim light of the club. Looking at him from a distance or in photographs hadn't prepared her for the impact of him so close. His focus was like a heavy weight centered in her chest. The small smile that tipped up his lips told her that he liked what he was seeing.

He was dressed all in black. His tight jeans hugged him like they were tailored to fit every toned inch of his legs. The henley shirt he wore strained taut over his impressive muscles. The only color on him were the patches that decorated his motorcycle club cut. Highdive, Sergeant at Arms was embroidered in red on his chest proclaiming his road name and position within the Dark Sons.

"Well, Luna. This is a surprise. I've seen you around the club, but never participating in a scene. I wasn't sure if you were a sub."

"I wish to submit to you, Master H." Diana hesitated but decided complete honesty was needed. "You should be aware, I've never been in a scene."

He raised an eyebrow. "Do you mean you've never been in a scene here, or at all?"

"At all."

He sat back crossing his arms in a gesture that could be interpreted as distancing, but his eyes never left hers. "I don't usually scene with beginners. They tend to get emotionally attached. Why should I make an exception for you?"

Diana tried to hide her smile at his unnecessary concern. Emotions had been beaten out of her at an early age. They were an inconvenience in her line of work, but that wasn't something she could share. This man intrigued her and woke within her a desire for the most carnal of experiences. Unfortunately there was no room in an assassin's life for anything as complicated as a relationship.

"I'm a blank slate. A puzzle without a picture. I'm not looking for anything other than discovering how this," she gestured to the activities going on around them, "fits into who I am. I'm not looking for anything but a skilled Master to spend a few sessions with."

"That doesn't answer the question." He raised an eyebrow. "Every man and woman who has earned the title Master at this club is skilled."

"I understand that." She shook her head. "The truth is complicated and simple at the same time. Although I'm willing to submit physically, I don't think I'm capable of doing so mentally. You don't seem to require that from your partners. If I'm wrong about that I'll apologize and leave you to your usual playthings."

It was a calculated risk to lay everything out there. She could have pretended to submit, she had been trained to fool even experts into believing whatever lie she wanted. But that would've been counterproductive to what she wanted to achieve.

His eyes had flared with interest. She had known he would see her words as a challenge. They weren't. She couldn't risk letting herself be that vulnerable. In another life maybe she would have been tempted to want something more, but the reality of her world made it impossible.

He ran a finger down her cheek and she enjoyed the rough feeling of his skin against hers.

"You are more confident than most new submissives. Your file says your only hard limits are blood play, bodily fluids, and permanent marks. Are you really interested in everything else, or are you just ignorant of what I could do to you with that much freedom?"

His threat sent chills down her spine. She had meticulously researched every item on the limits list. "I know what I've agreed to. I don't know if I'll enjoy any of it but that is what safewords are for and why I chose this club and you."

He stood and she had to tilt back her head to continue to look at him. This close, his large body was intimidating but even without her weapons she wasn't scared. Excitement had her nipples tightening as he walked around and stopped behind her. She felt completely exposed to him as she arched back trying to keep her gaze on him like he had ordered.

"But what is it you want from me? I've seen other Doms approach you. Is it ropes that interest you?"

The idea of letting someone tie her up both appealed and terrified her. She'd spent most of her life making sure she wasn't vulnerable, and maybe that was the problem. She thought over what had drawn her to him.

"I'm not sure you'll like my answer."

"Is that so? Stand and present."

His order was harsh. Cold in a way that settled something inside her. No emotion. A direct order. The chaos that so many people thrived in made her uncomfortable. She stood and clasped her hands behind her back in the way she had seen his previous submissives do. He towered over her, she was 5'6" in bare feet and he was 6'.

He ran his hands down her arms, readjusting her position until she was clasping her elbows behind her back and arching in such a way that her breasts were thrust forward. He circled back to her front looking over her body with a heat that was almost tangible.

"Your statement makes me want to know why even more."

It was tempting to craft a lie but Diana had promised herself in this one endeavor to be as honest as possible. She might not be able to give him her real name, or any truth about what she did outside the club, but she could give him this.

"I picked you because you are a focused, calculating, selfish perfectionist."

Master H crossed his arms, his eyes narrowing. "Selfish?"

She had known he wouldn't like that adjective but it was the one that had drawn her to him the most. "Your partners don't feel pleasure because they want to, they feel it because you want to see if you can make them feel it. You find pleasure in controlling a sub completely. Pleasure or pain, it doesn't matter, as long as you are deciding exactly what they are feeling. Once you know all their buttons they become uninteresting."

"And that appeals to you? Knowing that I won't do a scene with you again once I learn your buttons?" His smirk was sexy as if he found her amusing.

"Yes. Because then I'll know what they are, too and won't need you anymore."

His chuckle was dark. "That easy? You just want to use me to find out what trips your trigger. And what's in it for me then? Since I'm so selfish."

She wanted to growl in frustration, but bit back on the urge. She gave him her final truth, which would either tempt him with the challenge or send him scurrying away.

"I'm twenty-nine years old. I've had multiple partners of both genders and never once had an orgasm. If nothing else it would be appreciated if you could show me what that feels like."

"Never? What about masturbation?"

She shook her head. Solo exploration always ended up with her remembering something else she should be doing and giving up before finishing.

"Could you be asexual?"

She shrugged. "I have thought about that but I get aroused by men and other sexual things."

"What kind of sexual things?"

"Porn, erotic stories, being in a club like this. I don't know, the usual." She hadn't expected this line of questioning and that made her uncomfortable. Being this honest with someone was scarier than she had imagined.

Highdive had become an obsession, but she had only pictured him scening with her, not all this talking. Talking meant thinking and that was the opposite of what she wanted.

She had never had any trouble seducing a man in the past, but those had been parts of missions. Her ultimate goal had always been to either get information or kill the man once they were alone.

Admittedly, that might also be why she never orgasmed. Hard to lose yourself in sensation when you are thinking about how to break into their possessions or the different methods of killing them to make it look like an accident.

Trying to convince a man to have sex with her without deadly reasons should be easy. Unfortunately, it seemed she wasn't good at being attractive without the hidden goals. Maybe if she just pretended she was going to kill him after they were done this would be less awkward? Or she could just go home and work out her frustration on the punching bag.

"Do you do that a lot?"

Diana focused back on Master H. "Do what?"

"Lose focus."

Diana bristled. She had held her position and his gaze the whole time. "I never lose focus. I always know what's going on around me."

"Is that so? Because your pupils call you a liar."

She ground her teeth. How dare he challenge her ability to stay aware through anything. She had memorized complex images while being tortured during her training.

"There are twenty people in this room, three of them staff. In the booth to our right a man is getting a blowjob and during the time you accused me of zoning out the waitress picked up a tray with two whiskeys and a beer on it. I can tell you what every person in this room is doing right now if you'd like." She glared at him. "I don't lose focus."

Master H tilted his head back and laughed.

"Your focus should be on me and not on what anyone else is doing."

Highdive studied the woman in front of him with a hunger he hadn't felt in a long time. He had been ready to walk away thinking she was just looking for a Dom to treat her like shit. But if she was telling the truth, and he thought she was, the challenge of finding a way to get her to relax enough to come would be an interesting diversion.

Her observations about him were more accurate than he preferred to admit. He had noticed her before, she was hard to overlook, but had always assumed she was either a Domme or just a voyeur. Luna's body was a perfect mix of toned muscle and just enough curves to keep her appearance from being masculine. Her chestnut hair held amber highlights that were reflected in her eyes that were so light the color was almost gold.

Seeing her kneeling naked in front of his table had been a pleasant surprise. Standing on display she was a work of art. How inept had her previous partners been to not satisfy this beauty?

"I can focus on you and my surroundings."

"Already arguing with me?" Highdive raised an eyebrow.

Color brightened her cheeks and he didn't think this woman often blushed. Her observations about her surroundings told him more than she guessed. Hyper-awareness was usually the result of trauma or training. Since her file didn't have the mark they used to denote military or law enforcement he was guessing something had happened in her childhood. Breaking her out of that state once would be easy enough.

Training her to let go regularly so she could enjoy any type of sex, would take time. It would be a challenge. Something he hadn't had with a woman in a long time.

"I'm sorry, Sir."

"Accepted." He paused for a moment, getting his thoughts

together. "Reaching climax is the ultimate release of control. No matter how prettily you kneel. I don't think you've ever given up control to anyone. I have a proposition for you." A plan formed in his mind.

"What do you want?" She looked up at him with suspicion in her eyes.

Her wariness spoke volumes. Trust was an issue. Even though he was confident that everything she had said was the truth it was only the smallest portion of the picture. Usually after reading a woman's file he knew everything he needed to know.

The essay style questions revealed more than most people believed. Word choice, sentence structure, which questions had long answers and which were barely answered exposed hidden desires and needs. Her answers had left him with nothing but more questions.

They were dry statements of fact lacking any adjectives or expression of emotion. If Highdive hadn't seen the raw need in Luna's eyes when she first looked up at him he would have thought her a reporter or student researcher, not someone who craved submission. For the first time in his life he wanted to get inside a woman's head, not just her body.

Maybe he was a fool infected by the fact that so many of his Brothers were settling down that he wasn't as adverse to the possibility anymore. Or maybe it was the fact that he had been watching her for months and the puzzle she represented was too much of a temptation. The fact that she didn't want a commitment from him or an emotional attachment was a challenge he wanted to overcome

"Give over control to me. I will make sure your focus is only on me and what you are feeling. But only the first orgasm is free."

Her surprise was only evident by a slight widening of her eyes. She held the position he had put her in perfectly with not a single muscle twitch to betray what she was feeling. Luna's control was impressive.

"You want me to pay you?"

Highdive enjoyed the outrage that was subtle within her voice. Mind games had never been more than a small part of his play with others, but he found himself looking forward to matching wits with this woman.

"Not money, beautiful."

Her head cocked slightly and he could tell that she was running through possibilities in her mind. "Then what do you want?"

He traced the tiny lines that had formed on her forehead with the tips of his fingers, enjoying the smooth feel of her skin. A small wisp of hair had escaped from her braid and he tucked it behind her ear.

"In exchange, I want information." The look of horror that flickered through her eyes was interesting and only added to her mystery. "For every orgasm I give you tonight, and in what I'm guessing are the many nights to come. You have to tell me one thing about yourself. Doesn't matter how small it is. It just has to be something I don't already know."

"I don't understand. Why would you... I mean... why do you want to know about me?" Her stumbled words were signs that he was starting to crack her calm.

Had she played through in her mind how things would go? Was her earlier calm the result of calculated plans? She seemed to be so tightly wound that he guessed she had even practiced what she would have to say. Now she was thrown off-kilter by his unexpected request.

"I want to know about you. Learn what makes you tick." He ran his hand over her shoulder and lightly traced over the swells of her breasts. "Good sex isn't just about the physical. True pleasure starts in the mind. It's what makes dominance and submission so powerful." He chuckled. "So if you want to know what *trips your triggers* as you said, then I need to get in here." He ran his hand over her head and then slowly worked his palm down the center of her chest until he cupped the heat of her pussy. "Not just in here."

Highdive gave her shaved mound a light tap and she shivered. He placed his hands on her hips and it was almost like he could look into her eyes and see the thousands of thoughts flying behind her eyes. She was unique.

Though her pupils dilated and her lips parted in excitement her breathing was even. Calm and steady. He doubted her pulse was even slightly elevated. How strange was it that this inexperienced woman could stand naked in front of a practical stranger and maintain her calm appearance?

She had small scars on her arms and legs that might indicate that she had once been a cutter, but none of them were new. There were more scars on her back and sides. Some even looked like burns. Maybe an accident?

If she had been abused, he would have expected her to show fear as he loomed over her. He was twice her size, but that didn't seem to intimidate her in the slightest. Maybe she had some self-defense training? It was easy to see from her toned muscles that she stayed in shape.

Whatever had made her hyper-aware and shut off from the physical side of pleasure might be triggered by what he had planned so he would need to keep a close eye on her. The first time with anyone could be tricky, but she was so closed off anything could be held behind those closed shields.

He should probably not play with her until he knew more but she tempted every part of him to almost recklessness.

"I agree to your terms, Sir."

He chuckled at her very obvious wariness. Luna hadn't flinched when reminded of the extreme physical things he might do without limits, but sharing information about herself made her scared. What was she hiding?

"Are you sure? This is the last time I will ask. After that I will expect you to use the club safewords if you need me to slow or stop."

Her dark gaze grabbed him. Highdive could feel her intense earnestness. "I need this. I need you to show me what is possible. Thank you, Sir for agreeing, whatever the price."

The desire and longing in her words shot straight to his cock. That he was sure he could have named almost any price was heady. She wasn't just a young foolish girl looking for a walk on the wild side.

He had access to plenty of women who would do anything he asked for that frivolous reason. Sometimes it was because of his reputation as a master of Shibari, others because he was a member of the Dark Sons. Whatever the reason, it wasn't about him personally. Luna was no different.

If she wanted him to master her body then she would have to accept him learning things she didn't want to share. A plan settled into his mind.

Shabari was as much art as it was a way to restrain. The ropes that bound a woman's body in lattice like strands were a constant reminder that they weren't in control. Luna would need to have every ounce of control stripped away from her if he wanted her to submit and let go.

"Follow me."

He watched her out of the corner of his eye as he grabbed his bag from behind the bar. She was a mixture of coiled tension and outward calm.

He led her over to one of the more private stations near the back of the room. Usually he took his temporary partners to the ones in the center of the room. He knew the women who sought him out enjoyed the exhibitionism as much as they enjoyed what he did to them. They wanted people to know they had managed to earn a scene with him.

In this Luna was different. After the way she had blended

into the background for months it was obvious she didn't want to be center stage. With how beautiful she was it was quite an accomplishment that most nights very few had noticed her.

They would still have an audience, but he would do his best to make her forget there was anyone but the two of them in the room. If he thought she was ready to trust him he would have taken her to one of the private rooms for the first time. With the intense scene he had planned, he wanted her to have the safety of knowing that if she cried out her safeword there would be people around to make sure he stopped.

As they approached the suspension station he noticed how she was scanning the room. Almost like a trained soldier. Her gaze constantly moved, never resting in any one spot for more than a second. He could have almost imagined she was looking for danger, but she didn't walk like someone who was afraid of being attacked.

Highdive did a quick check of the suspension rig. He knew everything was well maintained but it never hurt to be safe. He intended to take away even the small amount of control contact with the ground allowed.

On the table he laid out his ropes in neat lines. He arranged the other items he intended to use next to them. That done, he turned back to face Luna who was waiting patiently in the presentation position. She was completely relaxed with a pleasant but neutral expression on her face.

Usually even experienced subs showed signs of nerves and excitement right before a scene. It was as if, instead of standing naked and vulnerable in the middle of a club, she was relaxed at home about to settle in for a night of TV.

What a fantastic mystery this woman represented.

"Come look at what I have laid out for you." Highdive led her over to the table. He watched as she took in first the ropes and safety scissors, then the nipple clamps and a Wartenberg wheel. Next was a Hitachi and a smaller vibrator. At the end was a furred vampire leather glove.

No reaction. No curiosity or fear. It was these small reactions that Highdive used to gauge how fast to move and how far to go. Her calm acceptance of all the items laid out meant this was going to be harder than he thought.

How could he push her further? He dug down into his bag and pulled out a specialty set of noise canceling headphones and mic as well as a blindfold. She looked at the headphones with confusion. Finally a reaction.

Luna looked up at him. "Sir?"

He smiled at the question obvious in her tone. Was she so comfortable with the other items because she had done research? Not many people knew how powerful cutting off the ability to hear was, but it was something he enjoyed. It was especially effective with subs who became overly concerned about their surroundings. He picked up the headphones and showed them to her.

"With these you won't be able to hear anything going on around you except for what I want you to hear." Highdive showed her the small throat mic that would be attached to him. "You'll hear my voice and anything else I play through the speakers." He picked up the blindfold. "You won't be able to see anything. I want your focus only on what you feel."

He stepped closer so their bodies brushed together. "I'm going to bind you so completely that even the smallest of movements are difficult. I'm going to take away all of your control so the only thing left for you is to be with me in the moment."

Her chest rose and fell in a slow rhythm. She wasn't breathing faster as he would expect but rather deeper and slower. It reminded him of his Brother Sharp when he was under stress. A sniper's technique of focusing under pressure. Where had she learned it?

"I don't see any floggers or paddles. There isn't anything on that table that could cause *real* pain."

From anyone else he would have thought that statement was a challenge. It was interesting how she emphasized the word real. What level of pain would she consider significant? Highdive didn't think she was a pain slut but only time would tell.

"No. I'm not a sadist. I only use pain to enhance my sub's experience or if they truly enjoy it. This first time isn't about exploring how much you can handle. I'm pretty sure you could take any pain I could give you and then some." The pleasure in her eyes at his statement confirmed his earlier thoughts. She didn't want pain but also wanted to prove that she wasn't weak. "This session is about getting you to let go. Forcing you to get lost in the sensations of your body to learn what it is that you've been missing. Only after I've taught you just how good your body can feel will I show you how much better it can be when you add a bit of bite to the experience."

The look of confusion on her face was almost adorable. But this woman's elegant beauty wasn't really made to be cute. She seemed to get lost in her own thoughts so he reached back and gave a sharp tug on her braid.

Her eyes refocused and snapped her attention back to him. Fire burned behind her gaze and he wondered how she kept it so well hidden. What must it be like to wrap yourself in control so tight that it smothered who you were?

Hopefully she wouldn't regret allowing him the opportunity to break through her shell.

"I want to make sure you understand exactly what's going to happen." He cupped her chin and made sure all her focus would be on his words. "I'm going to strip away all the perfect control you have wrapped around you like a protective blanket. I'm gonna take my time and make sure every inch of skin on your body is alive and humming with sensation. Then I'm going to make you come no matter how long it takes. Before your body or mind recovers I'm going to fuck you, bound and helpless. I'm not gonna stop until you come again and tell me something about yourself." He smirked. "If you keep your end of the bargain, maybe next time I'll show you just how much better it can get."

Watching her body shiver and her breath stutter was more satisfying than anything else she could have done in that moment. Being able to force unguarded reactions from her might be his new favorite activity. Doing so without even touching her was addicting.

She looked up and he could see hunger in her eyes. "I'd like that, Sir."

Her breath regained its even pace and he watched as she pulled her guards back up. It gave him an idea. He ran his fingers along her throat until he could feel her pulse. He was surprised by how calm and even the beat of her heart was. If he wanted to see her shatter he would have to break through that iron control she seemed to have over even the beat of her heart.

"I'm going to challenge you. I want you to count your heartbeats. I'll ask you for a number while we play and I'll expect you to give me that number."

"Yes, sir." The confidence in her tone confirmed to him that she didn't think anything could break her concentration.

The challenge would be exhilarating. He was determined to push her until she couldn't think straight. He smiled.

This was going to be fun.

Chapter 2

Sarcasm and Orgasms. Two things most people don't get. The ones who do are smiling right now.

D iana forced her breath to remain steady as she stood before Master H. Her decision to pick him was both genius and reckless. Already her mind was racing in directions that she had never considered at just the idea of what they were about to do. Did he want her to count her heartbeat to test if she could multitask or so that she would focus inward instead of on the room?

Trusting him enough to allow him to tie her up was already pushing her trust. But now he was going to take away her hearing and sight. Only years of training under harsher trials allowed her not to outwardly show how scared she was.

The noises of the room disappeared as he settled the head-phones over her ears. She could feel the vibrations of music and sound around her but all she could hear was an indistinct murmur. Closing her eyes to allow him to slip on the blindfold took a larger act of willpower than stepping into a firefight. Her skin came alive as her senses tried to adapt to the new conditions. The heat of Master H's presence behind her and the feel of the ground under her feet were the only things that felt real.

"Can you hear me?" His voice seemed to surround her with it's deep rich tone.

She took a deep breath to steady herself. "Yes, Sir."

"That's good." His hand ran up Diana's neck to the base of her throat. His fingers pressed in lightly. "Now I want you to start counting for me. 1...2...3"

The words were in time with her heartbeat and she relaxed into the count, taking it up mentally. The exercise was familiar. Something she had learned when training as a sniper. She could actually track time the same way. Forty-five beats to a minute was her normal at rest rate.

His hand slipped away and it was like she was adrift, alone. Only the cool floor beneath her feet to remind her she was standing inside the club. Air circulated around her in a way that she would have never noticed on a conscious level.

20...21

How many times had she counted her heartbeat while waiting for a target to show itself or while calculating the winds for the perfect shot? That was a number she really didn't want to think about. She barely kept from jumping when hands gripped her ankle. She forced herself to relax. The rope that was being wrapped around her leg was surprisingly soft. Master H's grip was firm as he moved quickly.

He had worked the binding around her leg several times all the way to her hip when he asked. "What is your count?"

"62, Sir."

Making herself vulnerable like this was foolish beyond belief. He wasn't really restraining her yet but that would come. She kept the count steady in her mind as she tried to picture what he was doing by feel. Around. Cross. Up. Sometimes around more than once. He began on her other leg.

Hundreds of possible outcomes had been considered. Every member of the club researched. She knew that no one who should be here tonight was associated with the many people who wanted her dead, but there was always a possibility that one of them could find her. She would be helpless.

82...83

These thoughts were pointless. Diana had chosen to do this and she would not allow fear to cripple her. Giving her trust to the man slowly wrapping her in rope was something she had decided. Second guessing herself wouldn't do anything but cause unnecessary worry. He was a well-trained Marine and his two friends, who were somewhere else in the club, were Rangers. If someone tried to hurt her, she needed to believe they could handle it.

"What is your count?"

"137, Sir."

She felt Master H start binding the rope around her arms and something inside her relaxed. It made no sense since he was finally restricting her movements. But it was like a comforting armor protecting her from her own worries. As if removing the choice of defending herself she was now safe to stop thinking about it.

Was this what the articles referred to when they mentioned the safety and comfort found in ropes? It wasn't a physical sensation, more a mental one where the more restricted you were the more comfortable you could become with not doing for yourself. Everything except for her counting and the brushes against her skin lost importance.

"Now for the fun part, beautiful. What's your number?"

"276, Sir." She hadn't noticed the number getting so high. Time was slipping away from her. There was a tugging at the ropes around her chest and hips. He had her breasts bound in a harness that was snug but not painful in any way.

"I've got you. I want you to lean forward and trust me."

Strong hands gripped her shoulders. She tilted forward till the rope held her from going any further. The hands left her shoulders. Her breath caught in her chest as, with a jerk, her hips lifted and she lost all contact with the ground. Stomach dipping she gave out a little squeak as she attempted to stretch her legs down to reach with her toes and instead started to swing.

Master H's chuckle made her want to glare at him but that was impossible with the blindfold. A second jerk and the tension brought her thighs up. She floated like superman in the air except her arms were bound behind her. She had been suspended before by her wrists but that hadn't been for fun. That had been a torture with her weight biting and the ropes painful.

317…318

Whatever he had done spread out her weight so it didn't hurt at all. In fact, it was almost comfortable. She forced away bad memories and let her mind settle. It was actually very peaceful. With all the rope surrounding her, it was like being face down in a hammock.

Master H's hands ran down the length of her body from her shoulders to feet. She felt ropes slipping in between her skin and the ropes at her ankles. Slowly her feet were pulled up until she hung in a cradle position. The only things that could move now on her body were her knees and head.

For long heartbeats she gently rocked in the position. Her breasts hung down and she could almost feel the blood flowing into them. As she relaxed her excitement grew. The air between her legs tickled and made her aware of how open she was. Master H could reach every part of her now and there was nothing she could do.

Tiny pricks of pain across her shoulder blades jolted her out of her daze. It continued down her back and across her ass. The object he was using on her was metal and sharp, it had to be the Wartenberg wheel. It wasn't really pain, more a shock that woke up every nerve the device passed over. As he circled her body she could feel the heat from his body like an aura.

"What's your count?" His voice was so sexy she wanted to find a way to wrap it around her.

"Mmh. 354, Sir."

Pleasure shot through her as he tweaked her nipple. As if the tweak was a starting bell, his assault on her body began. Soft fur then a slap, bite then a kiss. One sensation ran into the next, never pausing to let her settle.

He played with every part of her like she was an instrument he knew well. Her excitement built and she couldn't control her breathing anymore. It was like her pussy came alive with an aching need. She was empty and wanted to be filled. Diana tossed her head, more turned on than she had ever been in her life.

Her brain struggled to try to find a pattern in what he was doing, but it was impossible. Warmth covered one of her nipples and she cried out, almost losing her count as she felt him sucking on her nipple with hard pressure and an edge of teeth. Men had played with her breasts before but nothing like this with them bound in some sort of harness, it was like her breasts were alive and pulsing in time with her heartbeat.

429...430

He switched between her nipples and excitement built deep in her core. She wanted to see him, wanted to know what was going on. His fingers slipped between the folds of her pussy. "Oh please, yes," she moaned, surprised by her own begging words. Lightning raced up her spine as he brushed over her clit. How could something so simple feel so good?

443...439... wait no...444

Pain seared through her nipple as metal bit down and she screamed. It morphed into heat as he continued to rub her clit. Tension gripped her as something built deep inside her. She barely held back her scream as her second nipple was clamped.

"Don't hide your sounds from me, Luna."

He pulled down on the clamps and she screamed for him. A burning pleasure ripped through her and all she could do was feel. She threw her head side to side as he slapped her clit making the pressure inside her grow even more. Tugging and slapping in some rhythm she couldn't understand. Her clit throbbed and she was more aware of it than she had ever been before. The beat of her clit didn't match the pulse in her nipples which didn't match her heartbeat.

Her thoughts shattered like a crystal chalice dropped on stone. She was so close to something big that nothing else mattered but feeling.

"Master!" she cried out, overwhelmed by the conflicting sensations her body was giving.

"What's your count?"

She shook her head. A moment ago she'd known the number, or had she?

"I don't know." Her voice was hoarse. The admission of failure tore into her as she sagged into the ropes defeated.

Master H chuckled. "Good, then you're ready."

Pressure against her knees had her spreading wide. His mouth was warm on her pussy. An almost painful pleasure burned through her. So overwhelming. Why would anyone want to feel this out of control?

She needed more and less at the same time. His fingers slid inside her tight channel and she felt him slowly stretching her. Pleasure raced outward along her body and she thought she was going to come apart.

"Please Master!" She didn't know what she was asking for. But, she knew that she needed something because balancing on this edge was driving her crazy.

There was nothing left to do but give in. He could keep her riding the edge all night and nothing but her safe word would stop him. Her soul seemed to float above her body as she accepted that all she could do was feel.

"Come for me, Luna."

Master H sucked on her clit hard and the world exploded in light and pleasure. Like she had been blown apart but instead of pain there was nothing but ecstasy. She bucked against the ropes as her first orgasm rolled over her. She wished he had used her real name. That she had been honest enough to give it to him.

"That's it, beautiful. Come apart for me."

She was flying, her whole body buzzing pleasantly. There was no light and only the sound of his voice to ground her. He spread Diana's legs wider and the sound of his pleasure matched her own as he pushed inside.

He filled her in ways that she didn't know were possible. His breath was now heavy in the headset and she enjoyed the sounds he made as he claimed her with swift sure strokes.

It felt like her whole body was now a part of the primal rhythm. She swung against him and his hips snapped at the end of every thrust. Even though she didn't think it was possible, she felt that tidal wave of pleasure gathering inside her again.

"You're going to come again for me. I want to feel this pussy clutching me as you fall apart."

"Yes!" The word rushed out of her in a scream.

His cock brushed against a sensitive spot inside her on every single stroke. Not fighting it this time she let the orgasm burn through her. Pain flooded her nipples. He must have somehow released the clamps. White light filled her vision as she bucked as multiple waves of pleasure followed the pain. Master H roared through the headset and she felt him lose his rhythm before after a final thrust he stilled.

Silence wrapped her in a warm cocoon of peace. No thoughts surfaced to break the bliss of simply being in the moment. No plans. Nothing. She just floated, enjoying the stillness as it flowed over her.

Disappointment was bitter against her tongue as he pulled slowly out of her. He kept a hand on her, their connection was a warmth she never wanted to give up.

"I'm going to slowly lower you to the ground."

She smiled and giggled. The noise was foreign to her. Something she hadn't done since she was a child. Simple joy filled her.

This was why people lost their minds over sex. Why they made reckless decisions and betrayed their loyalties. She had used sex as a weapon on others but never really understood why it was so effective.

She was weak and vulnerable but none of that mattered while the pleasurable sensations freed her of doubts and worries. Even if in the back of her mind she knew it couldn't last, she wanted to stay this way forever.

The ground was cold against her sensitive nipples. Diana rested her cheek against the floor not wanting to be unbound. It was a silly wish but being released would mean their time had come to an end.

How could she make sure that he would be willing to do this again? The deal they had made replayed through her head. Master H lifted off the earphones and the sounds of the club came rushing back like a train barreling down on her. Along with the noise more coherent thoughts started to form.

He lifted off the blindfold and even the dim light of the club blinded her for a moment. She blinked up at him. Could he read how grateful she was in her eyes?

This was the first truly reckless and selfish thing she had ever done, but she didn't regret a moment of it. The look of concentration on his face was comforting as he began to unbind her, his motions slow and gentle.

Dianna licked her lips. "Master H."

He turned his gaze to her and his smile warmed her deep in her chest. "Yes, lovely Luna?"

She giggled. The sound of it so foreign, but perfect in that moment. What could she tell him about herself without risking her cover? Maybe if she shared only small bits of herself every time they met it could prolong his interest.

He would need to give her hundreds of orgasms before she would tell him anything big. Her determination and focus returned with that thought and she smiled.

"My favorite dessert is raspberry cheesecake."

Chapter 3

I miss you like a squirrel misses its nuts.

P*resent day*

Highdive glared at the text message on his phone. He took a breath then placed his phone down on the bar top at the Dark Sons' Clubhouse. There were only a few Brothers scattered around the big room that acted as a hub for the MC. Other than the Prospect on duty he was the only one currently indulging in a mid-afternoon drink.

Because of the partial lockdown, everyone was busy getting settled upstairs or in the apartments on another part of the compound. Highdive was supposed to stay here to coordinate if anyone needed anything. He stared at his phone sitting on the wood in front of him. The text message from Luna was the cherry on top of the shit sundae that had been his week. The universe seemed determined that absolutely nothing should go the way he wanted.

It had started with two of his Brothers, Hannibal and Ink, losing their minds over a woman who had a pathological need to put herself in danger. The week had continued plummeting downhill when she got in trouble with the Bratva and Hawk had made the decision to back her up even though his Brothers hadn't claimed her as their Old Lady. Now they were at war.

Highdive shook his head. He didn't really blame her for the war with the Russian mob. That had been inevitable. But it would have been nice to have more time to prepare. They could have avoided the war with what she had done if that lunatic Andre Petrov hadn't shot Hawk without warning in the middle of talks.

Planning for and dealing with this crap was all part of his job. He was the Sergeant at Arms, the Enforcer, the person responsible for the physical safety of all the Brothers. It didn't matter if the threat to them was internal or external, he was supposed to make sure they were prepared.

At times the task of keeping his Brothers safe felt impossible. Responsibility was a heavy weight on his shoulders. The only way to stay sane was to have a way to release that stress. Recently that had meant time with Luna at Dark Secrets. For the few hours he allowed himself to be with her all he had to worry about was their mutual pleasure.

Why couldn't Hannibal and Ink have found someone like her? Simple, uncomplicated, with no baggage to drag the club down. He took a sip of his beer.

At least he didn't think she had baggage. She never shared anything heavy with him and he never asked. Truth was, while he knew hundreds of tiny things about her, they had never discussed what her life was like outside the club. He had no idea what problems she might have. Her text had driven that home.

Luna: *I have to travel for work. I'll text when I get back.*

No details. No endearments. That was all it said. Not that he was expecting heart emojis and flowers. They weren't dating, just play partners. He had been waiting for the right opportunity to see if she would be interested in more, but the time never seemed right.

What did she even do for work? Highdive picked up his phone and scrolled back through all their texts. Times, dates, and outfit requests, nothing at all personal or emotional. He knew she felt emotions, though she would probably deny it. They had been spending longer and longer after a scene just sitting and talking.

He loved the simplicity of those moments. Aftercare had never really been his thing but the moments he spent learning new things about Luna were now some of his favorite memories. He loved all the strange little things he now knew about her. They talked about current events and movies. It was peaceful. But he also now realized it wasn't anything important.

How could he not know what she did for a living, or if she had any family? None of that had seemed important with her cuddled up against him.

He snorted at himself. Was he really getting sappy about cuddling?

It had seemed like a blessing that every time he said after-care was over she would get up, thank him with a kiss on the cheek, and walk out without ever glancing backwards. Simple, uncomplicated pussy. Exactly what he told his Brothers that he wanted. A zero drama woman.

How pathetic did it make him that the first time she wasn't available to him he wanted more? What would she be like outside the club walls? Her text was the first indication that she even had a job and that the job could take her away from the area. What would he do until she returned?

They'd never promised exclusivity. He could pick up someone else, either here at the clubhouse or at Dark Secrets. The idea turned to ash in his mouth. He didn't want anyone else. He wanted to find her and drag her back. She might not be safe with everything going on. Why hadn't he warned her?

Even though they weren't dating, they had been regular partners enough that someone in the Bratva could have found out about her. If they did, she would become a target. He wanted her here, where she would be safe, not out traveling God knows where. If she got hurt because she was completely unaware of the danger he would never forgive himself.

For the first time since he had gotten her number he hit the call icon.

The phone rang a few times and then a long beep to indicate voicemail. No message. Just a beep. Who the hell didn't have a voicemail message? He hung up without saying anything. Not sure if his impulse to call her had even been the right thing to do.

"Get me a beer," Hawk growled to the Prospect behind the bar as he slipped onto the barstool to Highdive's right.

The President of the Dark Sons looked tired. If anyone had asked Highdive a few days ago if this man could ever look anything but powerful and in control he would have said no. In his fifties Hawk always seemed like a force of nature. Unable to be affected by the day to day life that pulled everyone else down. Usually, if it wasn't for his gray hair, you would never know he wasn't in his early thirties.

Taking a bullet to his vest, the club going to war, and finding out that he might have a daughter out there somewhere was obviously enough to make him show his age. Andre Petrov had dropped that bomb of knowledge before firing his gun. His President had apparently been secretly hooking up with a crazy Russian assassin named Akula for years, and she had kept a big secret from him.

Highdive took a sip of his beer. All his Brothers had lost their minds. He'd felt smug as he watched the officers fall like dominoes for women with enough problems to fill a truck. No matter how messed up he had stood by his Brothers' sides and helped end any danger to the women they loved.

Now, they were all starting to settle down in American Dream style bliss. The only single officers left were him and Grinder, who just got promoted to Road Captain. He glared at the text from Luna. Who was he kidding? He wasn't single.

"Trouble?" Hawk's voice broke him out of his uncomfortable thoughts.

"Nothing you need to worry about, Prez." His problems weren't something for the club to worry about. Luna was just a regular hookup.

"The way you're glaring at that phone I'm guessing either a Brother isn't falling in line or you got pussy problems." Highdive glared at his President. Hawk burst out laughing. "No, shit? Hannibal said you had a regular woman but I didn't believe him."

"I swear the Brothers gossip worse than the Old Ladies."

Hawk took a sip of his beer and shrugged. "If she's serious enough for that glare, why haven't you brought her to the Clubhouse?"

"Not saying it is serious. Honestly never thought about it, but with the lockdown… I guess I don't want to see an innocent get hurt because of me."

"How long have you been seeing her?"

"We hooked up two months ago. But like I said, not serious."

Hawk raised an eyebrow. "How often do you hook up?"

"A few times." Highdive was uncomfortable with the direction the conversation was going. He was barely ready in his own mind to admit that things were anything but casual.

"Two months? Since you met? How often are we talking?"

"A few times a week. We meet up whenever I go to Dark Secrets."

"Shit, Highdive. You need to pull her in. I only see my woman a few times a year, and if I thought she wouldn't chop my dick off for trying, I'd have her safe under lockdown. Have the balls to admit she's more than just another one of your playthings."

"So you and Akula really are a thing?" Highdive had wondered. Until recently no one had had the stones to ask why their President never hooked up with any of the many willing women who panted after him. Most of them just thought he didn't want the distraction.

"My wife's name is Alena."

"You're married?" At that moment, if someone had walked in dressed in a clown suit Highdive didn't think he could have been more shocked. Never, not once, had anyone ever whispered that Hawk might be married.

"Yup." Hawk took a sip of his beer. The small smile that tipped up his lips showed he was enjoying shocking the shit out of his Enforcer.

"To a Russian assassin?"

"Yup."

"I don't even know what to say to that. How could no one know? When did you meet? How long have you been married?" Highdive knew he was almost babbling, but damn, that was a big piece of information without context. He should have been told.

"No one knows because you are the first person I've told." Hawk ran a hand through his hair. "Honestly don't know why I'm telling you now except that I guess you deserve to know why we're really at war. Why all the Brothers and their families, even your not so serious woman are at risk."

The guilt in Hawk's voice was more than he could take. "I was there when the nut job Andrey spouted his shit. Nineteen years is a long time to nurse a grudge. You didn't know she was engaged. You didn't do anything wrong."

"Oh, sleeping with her nineteen years ago was wrong, but not because she was engaged to another man." He swirled his bottle of beer. "It was my second mission as a SEAL. We were over in Afghanistan guarding some asshole who was selling information to the US from other assholes who wanted him dead. I was young and dumb, so when a hot Russian chick picked me up at the bar one night, I didn't think further than the end of my dick."

"I take it that your meeting wasn't just chance."

"Nope. She was using me to get information. The guy was scum, but it was my job to protect him. Fuck. I don't think either of us expected to fall in love but after a few days I was hooked. After the two weeks we spent together she probably could have convinced me to kill the guy myself, but she didn't even try."

"How did you find out she was using you?"

"We were getting ready to move him out of the country. I'd asked her to come back to the States with me. She couldn't travel with us, but I wanted her to meet me. Offered to pay all her expenses. Alena said she'd think about it, just about wrecked me that she didn't agree right off. That afternoon a sniper took out the guy. My squad was sent after the shooter. We're about to rush the building the shot came from and I see a woman in a hijab walking out calm as can be. No one but me notices her. But then no one but me would recognize those eyes."

"Did you confront her?"

Hawk chuckled. "No. And the only explanation I got at the time was a single word note."

"What did it say?"

"Sorry."

"How did you guys end up married?"

"I was out of the SEALs and had joined the Dark Sons Austin chapter. They were signing a truce with the Bratva and threw a party to celebrate. Imagine my shock when the head of the Stepanov family, Makail, introduces his daughter and favorite assassin, Alena."

"Fuck."

"That about sums it up. I managed to keep my head, but it was a close call. She snuck in to see me that night and an argument led to fucking. Somehow, three months later, we ended up in Vegas getting secretly married. Her family would kill both of us if they knew. I accept her for who she is even if that woman pisses me off as much as I love her. I wish I could say I don't believe that she wouldn't tell me we had a child. But if she believed it was the best way to keep us both safe, she would. I can't get ahold of her and it is driving me crazy. The last time we met she said her family wouldn't be an issue much longer, but wouldn't give details."

"Do you think she's okay?"

Hawk's face went cold and his eyes glinted with fury. "If she's not, I'll burn that fucking family tree down to its roots for her funeral pyre."

A chill washed down Highdive's spine. This man was their leader for a reason. They respected and trusted him with their lives. If he asked, every man here would run into the fires of Hell for him. Whether it was to take over a small country or wash his bike, he had earned their unswerving loyalty time and time again.

"You know we have your back."

All jokes and teasing aside this was why they were Brothers. The knowledge that you would never have to walk alone into danger. That all you had to do was ask and you would have an army at your side. He hoped it wouldn't be necessary, but if Hawk asked for help with vengeance, he would be the first to volunteer.

"Dark Sons for life." Hawk looked at him, the grim expression still firmly in place. "If you care for your woman, you pull her in. Patch on her back or not, this is war and no one is safe."

His President stood and strode off towards his office. With a sigh Highdive unlocked his phone. Luna wasn't going to like this, but Hawk was right. He needed to pull her in before anyone thought to use her as leverage to hurt him and the Club. How far was he going to have to go to keep her safe?

Chapter 4

Blood may be thicker than water, but in my family that is only
true when it is spilled on the floor.

The smell of spilled blood was something Diana was
all too familiar with, so she wasn't surprised when
she passed the first body. The marble floors of the
South Carolina mansion would probably be easy enough to
clean but she was glad it wouldn't be her problem. By the time
she found the fourth body sprawled on the stairs with a broken
neck it was easy to piece together that she probably wasn't
going to be needed, but she kept her weapon out and ready.

The screams and Russian curses coming from the upstairs
bedroom made it clear that someone wasn't having the
relaxing vacation this place was probably designed for. She
took time to clear every room before heading to the source of
the sounds not wanting anyone to sneak up on her. Nine dead
Bratva soldiers. It would have been an impressive count if she
hadn't known who was responsible for them.

When the Master bedroom came into view Diana was surprised to see her Uncle Arseney bruised, bloody, and tied to a chair. His back was to her and his attacker was nowhere to be seen as if they had conveniently stepped out. She snorted.

She would much rather be back in Colorado enjoying some private time with Highdive. Instead she was here with no clue as to why, or what was going on.

"I haven't fallen for obvious traps since I was nine years old," Diana called out. "You said you needed my help. Then vanished. I've spent the last month chasing you across the globe. I'm not in the mood for your games."

"Sestra!"

It had been almost a year since Diana had seen her half-sister. When Alena stepped out from behind the door she looked just like she had the last time they'd met, including the blood splatters barely visible on her black clothing. Looking at her was like looking into her own future. There were over ten years separating them in age and, though they had different mothers, they both took after their father in looks.

It was a good thing Highdive had never met Alena or he would have figured out that 'Luna' was hiding much more than just her real name. Not that that would matter anymore. After going radio silent for over a month she doubted he would be happy with her. After sending her initial text telling him she was leaving, she had turned off that phone to avoid the distraction of the temptation of contacting him again would be.

Silver highlighted her half sister's hair, but that was the only indication that she was now almost forty which was practically ancient for a woman who worked as an assassin. Her sister was the only person Diana trusted without hesitation. They hadn't known about each other growing up but the woman had found her nine years ago and helped her escape the influence of the family.

Since then they had tried to stay in touch, so when Alena had texted saying she needed help Diana hadn't hesitated. The two women hugged and ignored the cursing man tied up in the room.

"You could have told me how to find you." Diana smiled as they broke apart.

"Yes, but the price on my head is so high now that I wasn't sure you would come."

She gave her sister the look that comment deserved.

"*Is that you, Diana? You will let me go this minute,*" her uncle gasped out his demand in Russian.

So many questions ran through her mind it was hard to know where to start. As the bastard child of a crime lord, Diana had been treated as disposable from her first memory. A tool for the family that was only valuable as long as it was useful. But Alena was the cherished daughter, devalued because she was a woman but still important.

What had happened to turn her against the family? Or was this a job for her father? Alena usually wouldn't call her in for official Bratva business because feelings still ran high over her desertion. There was still a kill on sight order out against her. Diana walked around to study the man who had been responsible for killing her mother and placing her in specialized training.

As a child her uncle had seemed bigger than life, but sitting there beaten and bloody he was no different than any other desperate man. She had avoided seeing anyone from her childhood these last nine years. Maybe that had been a mistake. Seeing them again might put an end to her occasional nightmares. Especially if they ended up dead.

"*Why should I do that?*" She didn't often speak Russian anymore. Over the last few years she had worked hard to remove any trace of the language from her speech, wanting nothing to tie her back to the people who had raised her.

He coughed and spat. *"Your sister has gone mad and turned on the family. Kill her and I will see you raised up in her place."*

Diana looked over at her sister who was rolling her eyes. "What did they do?"

Alena might not have loved her family in the traditional sense, but she was loyal. She had to be since they held her daughter's happiness and safety over her head. Something must have happened for her to finally decide to break away in such a spectacular fashion.

"Papa decided that marrying off Nadya to the Pakhan of the Vasiliev family is more valuable than the loyalty of an aging assassin."

Diana winced. Yes, that would do it. Her niece had been pampered and raised in the equivalent of a gilded cage. They had tried to make sure she could defend herself but the girl had never had to survive the harsher sides of life. Their father might be a powerful man, but he was sometimes an idiot. Her chaotic sister was often a mystery, but only a fool would under-estimate the lengths she would go to protect her child.

"Isn't he over sixty?"

"Sixty-eight. His last two wives died conveniently under mysterious circumstances when he developed an interest in someone younger."

Her uncle started cursing them and all women, in general, in Russian. Diana sighed. This was going to be bloody.

"What do you need me to do?"

"Our dear uncle knows where Nadya is being held until the wedding. Help me find her and take her back."

"And what about her future groom?" Her sister and Nadya were the most important part of her life. She would do what was needed to help, but two women alone taking down two Bratva families was a tall order.

"I spoke with Vasiliev, he wants control of Stepanov

resources. He doesn't care how. Through marriage or Papa's death."

That made things much easier. Diana crouched down so she was eye to eye with her Uncle and let ice fill her voice.

"I guess we're going to find out who has the better training, Uncle. You at resisting torture or me at extracting information."

"Did you have to kill them all?" Nadya's voice came clearly through the earpiece. Her niece seemed surprised but not horrified, which was a good thing.

Diana disassembled her Barrett M95 sniper rifle, stowing it away for later disposal. Getting the location in New York where the girl had been held had taken less than an hour. Creating the plan to break her out took several days. But the assault on the remote cottage in the woods had lasted less than five minutes.

"Your *tetya* killed more of them than me. Which she will no doubt gloat over," Alena said with exasperation in her voice.

"I am not the showboat you are, *Akula*," Diana shouted over to where the two women were exiting the building. Her sister's moniker was well known throughout the underworld. She had been the stick their father used to beat his enemies into submission. Well known and feared, her name meant Shark.

The people who hired Diana referred to her as *Tishina*, or the English version of the word Silence. When she had been under the family's direction she hadn't been allowed to speak. Since then she continued the practice with her customers and rarely met them in person. Only the really powerful knew who she was and respected her wish to remain unknown. The rumor that to hear her speak was to know you were going to die amused Diana to no end.

"Aunt Diana?" Her niece turned and ran to her with a smile on her face.

The scene around them wasn't ideal for a family reunion. Five men lay sprawled dead on the lawn little left but a bloody mess where their heads used to be. Inside, lay three more dead, one from a shot through the window and the other two Alena had taken out. A normal nineteen year old would be freaking out. Unfortunately, although Nadya had been pampered growing up in a penthouse in Manhattan, she hadn't been sheltered from the horrors of what life in the Bratva meant.

Diana stood and opened her arms, welcoming the girl with an enthusiastic hug. Her niece had a black eye that was fading, but other than that seemed unharmed.

"Who hit you?" If the man who had done this wasn't already dead they might have to make a special trip to fix that.

Nadya looked down and shrugged. "*Dedushka* didn't like me saying I wouldn't get married."

The look of icy rage on Alena's face was enough to send fear shooting down her own spine. If there had been any chance that her sister would hesitate before killing their father it was now gone. Not that there had been much of a chance of that. Diana had learned that her sister had been a very busy woman the last few weeks. She had killed most of their father's brigadiers and the family was in chaos trying to hold things together. Those still left were either at his side or just waiting for the signal to switch their loyalties.

"You don't worry about that anymore, little rabbit." The gentle emotion on Alena's face as she ran her hand down her daughter's dark hair made Diana smile. "Your mama will fix this all."

The two women looked so alike, no one would mistake

their relationship. Nadya had her father's blue eyes and cheek-bones but everything else was from her mother. Stepanov genetics were dominant in most things.

"You're going to kill him aren't you?" The sadness in the girl's voice surprised her.

"*Da*. It is long past time."

Nadya raised her chin and took a deep breath as if steadying herself. "How can I help?"

Diana would have laughed if she didn't know it would crush the girl. She had the spirit of a warrior but none of the training something like this would take. Alena shook her head.

"You will go with *Tetya* Diana to your father. The two of them will keep you safe."

Wait, what?

"You never mentioned taking Nadya to Hawk." Dread pooled in the bottom of Diana's stomach. She had known it would be her responsibility to keep her niece safe but had thought they would use a safehouse or something. Never once had returning to Colorado come up in their discussions.

"I finally get to meet him? Like for real?" The hope and longing in her niece's voice was like a knife to her gut. The girl had grown up knowing that her father knew nothing about her. Until a few years ago Alena had kept his identity secret from everyone. Only after the girl turned sixteen and under-stood what would happen if she ever let the information out had Alena shared pictures and stories with her daughter.

Diana hadn't agreed with the decision. It felt like a cruel torture to know who he was and not be able to reach out to him. But it hadn't been her call. Now, if she refused to take the girl to Denver it would be her fault Nadya didn't meet her father.

"Yes. Someone told him about you. Not much but enough. If I don't send you there I'm sure he'd find you soon on his own. Between him, his Club and your aunt it would take a large army to get to you. I need to know you are safe so I can do what is necessary."

She was so screwed. Diana cleared her throat. "There may be a problem with that plan."

Both women turned to her with identical surprised expressions. Embarrassment wasn't something she was used to feeling but the heat of it was probably coloring her cheeks. How the hell could she explain without going into too much detail.

The last few months had been the happiest of her life. Even knowing it couldn't last she had let herself get lost in the time she spent with Highdive at Dark Secrets. He had given her so much pleasure that she'd come to crave it like caffeine. But it was those moments of peace on the couches in the after-care area that she would miss the most. Talking about everything and nothing. Forgetting for just a little while all the blood that was soaked into her skin.

"What is the problem?" Alena asked.

"Remember how you asked me to watch over Hawk and his Brothers when you had to go out of the country and you thought Andrey was up to something?"

Her sister looked puzzled. "*Da*. He was using that idiot to start trouble with the Dark Sons. You called me. I came back and fixed it. That was almost six months ago."

"I didn't exactly stop watching them."

Nadya giggled. "You've been stalking my dad?"

Diana shook her head. "Not your father."

Her sister got a wicked smile on her face. "Oh, little sister you have been keeping secrets. Which of his Brothers caught your spying eye?"

There was no way out of this now but to tell the truth. At least as much of it as was appropriate in front of her niece. "Highdive."

Alena threw back her head and laughed. "I never thought

you would go for the muscle bound soldier type. Did you actually let him see you?"

"Yes," she hissed through clenched teeth.

"How much of you did you let him see?"

She glared at her sister then threw a glance at Nadya. "Enough that this is going to be awkward."

"And he is still alive to tell the tale?"

Diana might have been offended at the insinuation, if it hadn't been a reasonable statement. Her sister knew that most of her previous lovers had been taken as part of a job and usually ended up dead before or soon after they got intimate.

"Ewh." Nadya made a gagging noise. "Please tell me you aren't like a praying mantis."

What was the girl going on about? It took a few moments for Diana to realize the girl was talking about how female praying mantises bit the heads off their partners while having sex. She started to deny the fact then tightened her lips around the lie. The comparison wasn't all that far off from reality.

Her niece threw her hands up in the air. "I don't want to know. Do you two have a car somewhere?" She gestured around the lawn. "I know you don't probably even notice but it is kind of creepy sitting here talking among dead bodies. I want to leave."

Alena handed her daughter a set of keys. "We're parked a mile down the road. We'll be right behind you."

Nadya headed off in the right direction and they followed just out of earshot. Neither of them were willing to let her out of their sight. Surprises could happen even in the middle of nowhere.

Her sister's voice was quiet when she asked, "Do you care for him?"

Did she? Caring for people was a weakness she didn't allow herself. Up until recently she had only cared for the two women now walking through the woods with her. Honestly she hadn't thought she could care for anyone but them. What she had with Highdive was fierce and wonderful. It was supposed to have been nothing but an experiment.

"He doesn't know who I am. He thinks my name is Luna."

"That's not what I asked."

It wasn't but she didn't have a good answer to the question. "He is an intense lover. Smart. Confident."

"Sometimes that is all it takes." Alena shook her head. "Do you think he will be a problem once he knows the truth?"

"Not unless he thinks I'm a danger to his Brothers. But if I take Nadya there and he finds out who and what I am, what we had will be over." The sadness in her own voice surprised her. It was inevitable and she had avoided thinking about it. Admittedly she had never considered the possibility that she would have to tell him about what she did when they weren't together. How would he react?

"She could go on her own—"

"No. She needs protection. No lover, no matter how good, is worth that risk."

Alena knocked her shoulder into Diana's as they walked. "You never know. Maybe when this is all over we can both get our men."

Diana shook her head. Her sister was definitely the optimist between the two of them. She just hoped he didn't hate her once the truth was revealed. Her life was rarely dull but this was going to be a kind of excitement she didn't enjoy.

Chapter 5

The only way to never be frustrated is to never have expectations.

Highdive scanned the bar of the Clubhouse. The room wasn't very full but he was on high alert. The knowledge that the more than thirty men here were killers from other MCs, local gangs, and the Mafia had his skin crawling with the need to keep an eye on every one of them. The fact that these men were supposed to be their allies had no impact on his sense of unease. He only trusted the twenty Dark Sons Brothers who were here; no treaty or agreement would change that simple fact.

He had recommended that they meet with each group separately so they could cut down on the risk, but Hawk had overruled him. The war with Andrey Petrov had escalated in the last few days and they would need all the help they could get to finish things quickly. Something was going on inside the Stepanov Bratva but no one was talking about what that was.

The feared attacks on a national level hadn't happened. But the asshole who had shot Hawk was assembling an army of almost a hundred men on a compound north of Denver and no one had any doubt he was going to cause trouble for the Dark Sons, but exactly how was a mystery. Even their contacts within law enforcement were stumped. It was as if the man was trying to form his own organization here and using the destruction of the Dark Sons as his opening move.

So far his Club had been lucky with only property damage and minor scuffles resulting from their conflict. But yesterday a few of the Old Ladies had been driving home from shopping when they were attacked by three SUVs full of men with automatic rifles. If it hadn't been for quick thinking and some fancy driving on Val's part, she, Pixie and Tari would have died.

In a few minutes he and the officers would be meeting with the heads of the different organizations present to work out how to take the crazy Russian down. The plan he and Tek had come up with was solid but it counted on overwhelming numbers and outside assistance. Highdive didn't like the odds that everything would go to plan.

"Highdive," Hawk shouted to him from over by the pool tables where he was standing with Tek, the Club's Secretary and Grinder, his best friend and the Club's Road Captain.

This room was made for parties not privacy. It was a giant room only sectioned off by the presence of the bar and several seating areas. They would have to go into Church to meet with the leaders. He hated the idea of outsiders in their private space but it couldn't be avoided.

Highdive strode over to see what his President wanted. "What's up?"

"Finally got a message from Akula." Hawk's voice was low but he could still hear the frustration.

Hawk's woman had been MIA for over a month causing

the man to grow angrier every day. Highdive sympathized with his President. Luna had vanished as well. That was a mess he had no idea how to unpack and he didn't have time to think about it now.

"What did it say?"

"That she is sending me a package today and I need to keep it safe." If Hawk clenched his jaw any tighter he thought the man might need dental work.

"That's it?" Highdive asked.

"Yup. It's like she has a sixth sense for the worst possible timing."

"Do you know if she's in town or likely to show up with the package?"

Hawk chuckled. "She's not going to show up or call because then she would have to actually talk to me."

Tek cleared his throat. "Cami and I tried to trace the email but all we could figure out was it was sent from a temporary account set up from a burner phone that is no longer active. I've let the Brothers on duty know we are expecting something. Hopefully it won't come until after our guests have left."

His Brother was a computer genius but his Old Lady made him look like an amateur. If they couldn't find anything, there wasn't anything to be found. It probably wasn't the time to ask but he couldn't help himself. "Anything new on Luna?"

Tek gave him a sympathetic look. "No. Still no idea what her real identity is. She's a complete ghost. Cami is taking it personally but even she found nothing."

He had broken down after a few days with no responses to his texts and asked for help tracking her down. At the time he had been worried the Russians might get to her. Finding out that the woman he had been spending time with for months had used a fake identity to get membership at Dark Secrets had been an unpleasant surprise.

He had spent many sleepless nights trying to figure out if

she had been using him to get access to the Dark Sons. But the simple truth was she never asked him about anything going on at the Club. Never even suggested they meet anywhere but for scenes. He had even searched everything he had for bugs or signs of tampering. Nothing.

She was a ghost that he didn't have time to hunt down. But he would. When this mess was over he would find her and discover why she had come into his life and then disappeared without a word.

Hawk pinched his nose and shook his head. "Knowing my woman the package could be anything from Petrov's battle plans to a crate of rocket launchers. When I get my hands on her she isn't going to sit right for a month." He sighed and looked around the room. "Everyone's here. We need to get this meeting started before someone says the wrong thing and we end up with a gunfight in the middle of the Club."

Tek and Hawk strode off and Grinder gave him a hard look that he knew too well. He was about to get a lecture. "You've got to stop beating yourself up over that woman."

The two of them had met in the Marines and been discharged at the same time. They had prospected the Dark Sons together and had been close ever since. Grinder was usually the more relaxed of the two of them. Going through life as if it was one big party, but when things got rough there wasn't anyone better to have at your back.

Unfortunately their long friendship meant he wasn't fooled by his bland expression. Most of the Brothers thought he had a heart of stone and it was better that way. It made his job of being an Enforcer that much easier. It was his job to do the things that were necessary to keep them safe. Even if it was at the cost of his own happiness.

"She could be a risk to the Club."

Grinder snorted. "You aren't worried about that and we both know it. You may fool them," his friend nodded to the other Brothers around, "but I know the truth. She was good for you. Before all this happened I'd never seen you so relaxed. She's a mystery and you fucking love that shit. But if you don't get your head on straight, the distraction is going to kill you."

"You think I don't know that? I spend almost every waking moment focused on the Club so excuse me if I take five fucking seconds to ask for an update."

"That is not what I meant. Fuck, Brother. It is usually you ragging people about keeping pussy uncomplicated. You need to put her out of your head. Stop trying to figure out the lies and leave it be until later."

"I can't even say she lied to me, because I don't know what the truth is." Highdive ran his hand through his hair in frustration. "It's not finding out that bothers me. It's not knowing if she is okay. I protect people, I don't put them in danger. And I've either put her at risk by getting mixed up with her or put the Club in danger by getting mixed up with someone who was playing me. But yeah, I know where my focus has to be."

Getting Tommaso Minetti to get them the armor, weapons, and ammunition they needed in time. The mob family had been loyal allies for years and he didn't think they would balk. But the timeline was short and without the extra supplies the body count would be high. They needed to outfit almost fifty extra men from other Clubs to protect their interests while the Dark Sons focused on Petrov.

"Good." Grinder motioned toward the back hall. "Hawk is pulling everyone back."

It was time to see if they could make his plan work.

Chapter 6

The most dangerous animal in the world is a woman sitting in silence and smiling.

"**A**re we there yet?"

Tying up her niece and transporting her to her father in the trunk was becoming more appealing by the minute. Driving cross-country with a bored teenager would definitely be added to her list of forms of torture, though she wasn't sure how practical it would be. It wasn't the girl's fault really; the nineteen year old had just never learned patience or the beauty of silence.

"You know I kill people for a living right?" Diana said with a smile.

"Yes. I know. You're a badass. My mom's a badass. My dad's a badass. It's all *very* impressive." Nadya sighed dramatically. "Unlike me."

They were almost there, so Diana took a moment to look over at her niece. Nadya's hands were fidgeting with her new clothes as if they didn't fit correctly. It was obvious she was nervous. That morning the girl had spent so much time with her makeup and hair only threats of violence had gotten her out of the bathroom.

Comforting people was not something Diana was used to doing. But for her niece she would try. What would make a teenage girl feel better? Maybe compliments.

"You are smart, resilient, and beautiful. It is good that I taught you how to kill a man before you were eleven or you would have had to have more bodyguards."

Nadya laughed. "Mom actually taught me how to do that when I was nine."

"What?" Diana narrowed her eyes in mock anger, glad that the subject appeared to be distracting the girl. "Hmm. I thought you learned knife fighting a little too quickly. I can't believe you lied to me."

"We had just met. You were so bad at the bonding thing, I didn't want to hurt your feelings."

She chuckled. Normal relationships had always been a struggle. Friends could be a weakness and relationships impossible when she couldn't be honest. What she and Highdive had was the closest thing to normal she had ever tried and that was about to be destroyed when he learned the truth about her.

Diana sighed. "Was I really that bad?"

"You were."

They were both heading into an uncomfortable situation. The main difference was that Diana had created her own downfall by keeping secrets where Nadya wasn't at fault at all. According to Alena, Hawk was a good guy. He wouldn't hold his daughter responsible for what her mother had done.

"Your father is going to love you."

Nadya's laugh held a nervous edge. "You don't know that."

"Well if he doesn't, I point you back to the beginning of this conversation. Remember what I do for a living."

"You can't kill my father if he doesn't like me."

"Says who?" She probably wouldn't, but the teasing seemed to be relaxing her niece.

"Mom might be a little mad if you kill her husband."

Diana shrugged. "She'll get over it."

"Sometimes it's hard to tell when you and Mom are joking."

Diana gave her niece a small smile. It was good that they had managed over the years to allow the girl even the smallest amount of innocence. They never joked about their willingness to kill. The only people she would even hesitate to eliminate were her sister and niece. Her chest clenched for a moment. She also might hesitate for Highdive.

The gate to the Dark Sons' compound was on the left and she pulled up. The chain link gate was closed blocking the entrance to the compound, which was unusual. The man on guard approached them. He was wearing a Dark Sons' cut that said his name was Decaf. Diana gripped the gun concealed in the door before she rolled down the window. His smile was tight, but friendly, when he leaned down to talk to them.

"Sorry ladies. The compound is on lockdown. No one's allowed in. You'll have to come back another week."

What had happened to put them on lockdown? She knew the conflict between the Club and Andrey Petrov had been escalating. Could things have gotten so bad since she left that they were now at open war?

It was late afternoon and the parking lot at the front of the compound usually only had a few of the Brother's bikes. The place was now half-filled with vehicles like there was a party going on, but she didn't recognize most of the cars from her many scouting missions.

High-end blacked-out SUVs and lots of bikes. Should she come back with Nadya later? It would be a relief to put off facing Highdive, but Alena had been insistent that they go immediately. She glanced over at her niece. The girl looked like a spring wound too tight. Leaving when they were so close would be cruel.

She took a breath and locked down all her emotions. This was a job and she couldn't afford to be questioning things.

"Hawk is expecting us. I have the package from Akula."

Decaf raised his eyebrows and studied the two of them. He didn't seem to be confused by her words so her sister's message must have been passed on. Was it that he didn't believe two women could be the couriers? They would all be surprised when they found out who the package was.

Nadya looked like a typical fashion conscious nineteen-year-old girl. She wore artfully ripped jeans and a crimson top and designer boots. The whole outfit probably cost more than most kids' entire wardrobe.

Diana, on the other hand, was dressed for combat. Black BDUs, combat boots, a long sleeve, tight, black top and a long jacket designed to conceal enough weapons to handle most situations.

"Give me a minute." He stepped back from the car keeping an eye on the two of them and raised his cell phone to his ear. "I've got two women here. They say they have the package from Akula. What do you want me to do?"

The silence stretched and Diana wished she could hear what was being said on the other side.

"You're sure? All right." The man was obviously not pleased with what he was being told. He ended the call and slipped his phone into his back pocket before hitting a button on the panel next to him and the gate started to open. "Park your car over there. Clean will meet you by the front door and escort you from there."

Diana nodded and pulled forward as soon as there was enough room to do so. She parked in the spot that he had indicated. Worry over walking into the unknown tickled at the back of her thoughts.

"What's going on, *Tetya*?" Nadya's use of Russian showed more than anything how nervous she was. The girl had grown up speaking both languages but, like Diana, had worked hard to sound as American as possible from the time she hit her teenage years. The only time Diana used an accent now was when on a job posing as someone else.

"It will be okay." She would do everything in her power to make sure that wasn't a lie. Why had her sister insisted on this course of action? She thought the reunion could have waited until the violence was over. Trusting in her sister was hard.

From this close it was easier to tell the cars were of the armored variety. She hoped that this was just a private party, but the lack of half-dressed women hanging around said that was unlikely. The several obvious guards at the front door was also a strike against positive thinking since not all of them were Dark Sons.

Diana recognized one of the men as a low-level soldier for the Minetti family. This meeting was going to be so much more complicated than an awkward family reunion. If there were any of the higher ranking soldiers inside they might recognize her. Over the last several years she had done a lot of clean up work for the Minetti family in New York. While their Don loved her, she wasn't as popular with many of his soldiers since it was their messes she'd been cleaning. Men's pride were delicate things and having to be saved by a woman often bruised their egos.

"Until we get to talk to your father I need you to keep your head down and your mouth shut. There are people here who aren't friends. I don't want to have to start killing people because you piss off the wrong person."

Nadya raised an eyebrow. "I'm not a child. I can take care of myself."

Diana took a deep breath, teenage egos were almost as annoying as men's. "That attitude right there is the problem. You think this is about proving to me that you can fight. I need you to prove that you can keep your head. We are outnumbered and in a completely unknown situation. You're not the Bratva Princess anymore. No one will hesitate to hurt you if you mouth off and prick their price."

"I promise I'll be good." The girl's tone held so much exasperation that it was hard not to laugh. Diana doubted her niece even knew the meaning of 'good' but it was the best promise she was going to get.

They got out of the car and Nadya looked around at the place with wide eyes. The Dark Sons' compound was an interesting mix of impressive and functional. The Clubhouse was a two story structure that was a visual mix between a warehouse and a small apartment building. Two other large buildings were visible from where they had parked.

Diana knew one of them was a gun range that was also used for backup weapon storage. The other was a garage where the Brothers kept the spare vehicles. She had spent months memorizing the entire complex and it was like a strange sort of gated community.

Deeper in the property, blocked from view by the Clubhouse, was an actual apartment complex. The single Brothers and those on active duty lived there. Hidden near the middle of the grounds were single family homes where officers and some of the higher ranking Brothers with families lived. It was an amusing mini version of suburbia.

As they approached, a man walked out of the doors to meet them. She recognized Clean from her time spent watching the club. His average looks and non distinct personality made him perfect for going unnoticed. Which, of course, had made her take a closer look. His past was almost as dark as hers. He had been to the government what she had been to the Bratva. An assassin, a cleaner, or more generally a problem solver. Behind his unassuming demeanor was someone nearly as cold and deadly as she was.

He was Highdive's right hand when it came to taking care of the dirty work within the club. Hopefully she wouldn't ever have to go toe to toe with the man.

It was time to face the music.

Clean crossed his arms and looked the two of them over. His eyes held no interest in their looks, instead quickly scanning the places where the two might have weapons. Diana was impressed by the fact that he didn't seem to dismiss either of them as harmless. Under his assessment it was easy to fall into the cool persona that she used for business. She wasn't Diana anymore, she was Silence.

"You've got a package for us?" Clean's voice was clipped as if he didn't want to be talking to them.

Diana nodded and her eyes searched over the men at the door. She wouldn't be talking about anything in front of people she didn't know.

Clean held out his hand as if he expected her to hand over something. She just raised her eyebrow. Even if the package had been something that could be handed over she knew her sister's message would have made it clear that it would only be given to Hawk. Did the man think her a complete amateur? They stared in silence for long moments.

"Where's Hawk?" Nadya's voice was sharp and demanding and Diana wanted to strangle her as all the men's attention snapped to her.

Stepping in front of her niece Diana used her body to block their view. She kept her voice low so it would be hard for the men standing at the door to hear her. "I have very clear instructions, the package is for Hawk alone."

Clean's jaw twitched. "This isn't a good time. You'll have to come back."

It was tempting to take the offered escape. Unfortunately, they would only have the element of surprise once. If Andre had someone watching the Dark Sons' compound he would have recognized them both. Coming back later was asking for trouble.

"If we leave we won't be coming back." Diana kept her voice neutral as if she didn't care, but Nadya made a sound of disagreement. She turned and glared at her niece until the girl blushed and nodded her head.

"Fuck. This is not going to go well. Fine, follow me. Do not talk to anyone. Do not cause problems." He walked them inside the Clubhouse at a quick pace.

Diana looked around with interest. She had never actually seen the inside of the Clubhouse since all of her observation had been done from a distance. The place was impressive. The room they entered was large, open, and much cleaner than she would have pictured. To the right was an impressive bar that would have been at home in any high-end club. In the back of the room several pool tables were currently in use. Small seating areas were also scattered around and some of them occupied by dangerous looking men.

The Clubhouse could probably hold well over a hundred people for the types of parties she knew were common on the weekends. Right now, it only held around thirty men, all of them looking their way. Diana wanted to curse her sister's stupidity for not thinking of a better way to approach Hawk.

At least three of Minetti's men were here and she knew they recognized her by their hostile glares. She also recognized at least three other motorcycle club cuts and even men from some of Denver's worst gangs. The one thing that was completely absent from the room, other women.

The two of them had apparently stumbled on some sort

of gathering of soldiers. The lack of anticipation hanging in the room or any sense of purpose told her at least it wasn't a prep for something about to happen. It was probably some sort of treaty negotiation or strategy meeting.

None of the Dark Sons' officers were in the room, so she guessed they were in the back somewhere with the leaders of these other groups. On one hand, that was good news because she got to put off the coming confrontation for a few minutes. On the other hand, lower level members of criminal groups weren't always the smartest men. With the way Tony, one of Minetti's soldiers, was looking at her, a confrontation was likely.

Tony had tried for several years to push her buttons believing she just needed the right man to settle her down. They had become enemies one night when his pushing had crossed the line from words to touch and she had embarrassed him by taking him down in front of other members of the family. He had been banned from attending any meeting where she was going to be physically present because the Don didn't want her to kill him.

She pretended not to notice him as Clean led them to a table near a side hallway. It wasn't ideal for defense but she would make do. Diana only held out a small hope that Tony would do the smart thing and ignore her, so she needed to be ready.

Clean glared at them. "Sit here. Don't cause any problems." He stalked away down the hallway, hopefully, to get Hawk.

"What an asshole," Nadya muttered under her breath as she hopped up onto one of the pub style chairs.

Dianna snorted. "If you think that's being an asshole, we really have kept you too sheltered."

"Whatever." Nadya looked around the room, her eyes sparkling with mischief. "Is your boyfriend here?"

Diana shook her head and positioned herself so she could see the room better, but didn't sit. "Please take this seriously. Something's going on and I don't like it. Most of these men aren't from your father's Club. If any of them come over don't say anything, let me handle it. If things get physical you stay behind me no matter what."

"Aunt Diana, you're being ridiculous," Nadya whined.

"Promise me or we leave now," Diana growled.

She didn't want to scare the girl, but with Tony now heading their way it was likely things weren't going to go smoothly. All their intel said the men within the Dark Sons' Club were trustworthy but she had no such assurances on the rest of the people here. She felt like a guard dog who had been ordered to protect a small mouse from a room full of feral cats. She was good, but no one person could take odds this bad.

"I'll be good. I swear. I've waited nineteen years to meet my dad. Now that we're here, I don't think my nerves can take waiting another day."

Diana sighed. Her niece was under a lot of stress and wasn't used to it. Her own nerves about facing the man she had been seeing for months didn't help this whole situation. They were so far outside of her comfort zone they might as well be in another country.

In the past she had purposefully avoided situations like this. Her jobs were methodically planned; all alternatives accounted for. Order and preparation ruled her life. Not knowing how Hawk would react at meeting his daughter, or what Highdive would do once he found out she had misrepresented herself were huge wildcards. Throwing in the soldiers from several other organizations and the chaos would be extreme.

That didn't even take into account the stress that always came from being the only woman in the room. Intellectually people knew that women were the more deadly sex, but practically they were dismissed because of their smaller stature. Usually being underestimated was something she preferred. But here she needed to avoid killing so she couldn't take advantage of their ignorance.

"Be calm, little rabbit. Your father will come out soon and we can go somewhere safe."

"You know I hate when Mom calls me that." Nadya rolled her eyes. "Who's the guy coming over? He's looking at you like you stole his lunch money."

"He's someone I know from my day job. Tony doesn't like me much. Don't use my name or let him know we are related if you can help it."

"Okay, *Tishina*." The amusement in her niece's voice was overwhelming.

"Actually, how about you just not talk?"

Nadya shrugged and Diana didn't like the look in her eyes. But she didn't have time to deal with it. She needed all of her attention focused on the man approaching with a snarl on his face. She moved to place herself between her niece and the danger.

Most women would have called Tony handsome. He wore an expensive suit that was tailored so well only a practiced eye would notice the guns in holsters at his side. His Italian sharp, dark looks had fooled many women into believing he was a good guy. Until they found out he didn't understand the word, no.

"Tishina is that you?" Tony practically shouted though he was only ten feet away. "And here I thought my eyes were deceiving me. What is '*The Silence*' doing away from the bright lights of New York?"

His words were friendly enough but Diana knew them as the lies they were. She crossed her arms not answering with anything but a stare. Anything she said he would twist and try to turn it into a challenge.

He looked over her shoulder and surprise flickered through his eyes. Damn, he had recognized her niece. Nadya had been kept out of the limelight but not hidden. Since they were both from New York City she should have anticipated this

"Is that the Stepanov Princess? I thought you weren't their little guard dog anymore. It shouldn't surprise me that you're working for them again since you were always such a bitch."

The man really thought he was hilarious. Diana faked a yawn but kept her eyes locked on him. If this was the best he could do she would easily wait him out until Clean brought back Hawk.

"Go away, no one wants to talk to you." Nadya's words were dripping with the haughtiness she had learned from her grandfather.

"Don't talk to me like that, little girl. I heard your grandfather sold you for a few soldiers and some weapons." He leered at her. "I also heard you're a whore just like your mom. Maybe I'll take you in the back and show you what a real man is like before you're stuck sucking an old man's cock for the rest of your very short life."

Tony stepped to the side as if to make a grab at Nadya and Diana stepped with him blocking his access. What she hadn't expected was that her niece would come flying over her shoulder screaming in rage. The girl managed to tackle the man to the ground with the surprise move. Diana pulled her niece off of Tony with a quick move and shoved her behind her. There were several scratches welling blood on the Italian man's face.

"Stay behind me," Diana snarled and faced off against Tony.

The man had come up swinging, and she ducked under

the clumsy blow. She kicked out at him forcing him to back away.

Tony's eyes were filled with hate. "So you can talk, good. Now I'm going to make you scream in pain. Teach you the lesson I've wanted to for years. And then I'm going to do the same to the little whore Princess."

"I don't want to have to kill you." Well, that wasn't true, but it was always good to give a warning.

They were in an unfamiliar situation. Normally, she would have already pulled a gun and shot the man. But trying to keep the peace was an unfamiliar predicament. So she hesitated, expecting Tony to keep things within the bounds of a non-lethal confrontation.

Unfortunately, Tony didn't. Before she could react he had his gun out and pointed at her. Her world focused down to him, and that gun. She positioned herself so she was between Nadya and a bullet. Diana had been shot before and, as long as he didn't get lucky, if he fired she would survive long enough to make sure he didn't get her niece.

"Not so tough now," Tony mocked and stepped closer. "Your girl broke the rules when she attacked me, so I can do anything I want to both of you." The gun was pointed right at her head so she didn't dare move. "I'm going to fuck some humility back into you, bitch."

Diana gave him a cold smile, a plan forming in her head. "I'd heard that the only way you could get a woman into your bed was at gunpoint. I thought they were lying since you have that pretty boy face." She chuckled looking at his now bloody cheek. "Though I guess it's not that pretty anymore."

"*Puttana!*" He pulled back the gun to pistol whip her and she moved.

She ducked under the blow and grabbed his wrist in a twisting motion using his own momentum against him. As she circled with him, she swept his legs out from under him and wrenched the gun from his grip. He went face down onto the ground and she stood with the gun now under her control. She aimed at the back of his head. There was no time to hesitate. She pulled back on the trigger.

Someone grabbed her shoulder causing the shot to miss his head and end up hitting the floor instead. Diana spun, pointing the gun at her newest attacker, intending to take him out before returning her focus to Tony.

Chapter 7

People think I'm crazy, then they meet my family and realize
I'm not so bad.

There were many ways Highdive had pictured seeing
Luna again but he had to admit this scenario hadn't
even occurred to him. Staring down the barrel of a
gun, her eyes locked on his with a killer's gaze that felt like ice.
She was glorious. Dressed in combat gear, hair pulled back in
a tight ponytail, and not even breathing hard after taking
down a man who was almost twice her size. She was almost
sexier than when she kneeled before him naked and submissive. Almost. His cock pulsed it's agreement even though
Highdive wasn't sure if she was going to pull the trigger
or not.

"What the fuck is going on here?" Hawk's voice cut
through his daze like a heated knife.

He didn't have an answer for his President. The meeting
had broken up and Clean had come to tell them that the

courier was there with Akula's package. They had headed down the hallway to find out what the crazy Russian woman had sent them. The sounds of an argument had spurred them into moving faster.

They had come out to see Tony, one of the Minetti soldiers, holding a gun to Luna's head. Rage had burned across his skin at the thought of her in danger. The man had gone to strike her but before Highdive could do anything she had moved like a demon and taken him down. He had tried to pull her away so he could kill the man for daring to attack his woman.

That was where everything had gone odd. Luna had turned the gun on him and stared at him like they were strangers. It was as if they were caught in a frozen moment in time. Recognition finally entered Luna's eyes, but she didn't lower the gun. What the hell was going through her mind?

"Put the damn gun down, Diana," Hawk snarled.

How did Hawk know his woman? He spoke her name as if he not only knew her but knew her well enough to expect her to obey him. Highdive looked at his President with shock.

Luna, or should he say Diana, gave a shrug. She lowered the gun, ejected the magazine, and cleared the chamber before offering it to him. Her motions were practiced and casual. As if she didn't have a worry in the world, that fighting for her life was boring and routine. She looked at him and only the slight tightness around her eyes gave him any indication that she might be concerned. How much didn't he know about the woman who haunted his thoughts?

"Diana?" Highdive asked in a low tone as he took the weapon.

"Long story. Promise to tell you later." With those few words it was like the shutters dropped and her eyes iced back over.

She strode away to stand in front of the only other female

in the room. The young woman appeared to be around twenty. The two women looked as if they were related with similar dark hair and strong features. But the girl had an air of innocence about her that had never been a part of his submissive. Could the two be sisters? Why would she have brought her sister here? The idiot on the ground rolled over and stood.

"That bitch attacked me then her guard dog tried to shoot me. I demand to take them with us for punishment."

Tommaso Minetti stepped out of the hallway with a mildly interested look on his face. He was completely put together, as always, in his designer suit. He seemed to study his man then the two women.

Tony had scratches on his face. Neither of the women looked injured. There were very definite rules that covered what was and wasn't allowed when it came to violence during meetings like this. No one was allowed to start a fight except Dark Sons and their family. It was one of the main reasons they kept family and any hot head Brothers away.

Hawk looked at Diana. "Is that what happened?"

She gave Tony a look that would have made a sane man fear for his life. "Minus the fact that he threatened to rape her before she attacked him."

The growl from the Dark Sons in the room should have made the idiot Italian back down but he didn't. "There are no rules about what we say. Only what we do."

Tommaso looked at Hawk and gave a shrug. "They are your rules." The man didn't look happy with his soldier, but with so many outsiders around there was no way he wouldn't back his man.

If they let that dickhead take Diana and the girl with her every one of them knew what would happen. Bending the rules wasn't an option or they would never be able to hold a peaceful meeting again. Every asshole would try to test the boundaries claiming the rules were unclear. Highdive might be mad at Diana for keeping things from him but not to the point that he would let her be raped and killed.

Hell, he didn't want to see her hurt ever. The last few months she had given him something no other person had ever been able to. She had given him peace and a happiness that with time he was sure would have grown into more. Even weeks apart, knowing she had been keeping secrets, hadn't changed those feelings. Seeing this new bad-ass side of her made her even more attractive.

He had to do something to save her. But what? The rules were very specific. If she wasn't family then…

"She's my Old Lady. She's family." The wild idea was out of his mouth before he even processed the possible consequences. It was a solid plan at least for the short term. Everyone looked at him with the same look of shock which was good because no one noticed the disbelief on Diana's face before her cold mask of indifference settled back into place.

Tommaso looked at Diana with amusement in his eyes. "Is that true? You are his Old Lady?"

"What does it matter that I'm his Old Lady?" The quiet chill in her voice shouldn't have been sexy but it was. He was glad she was playing along though it wasn't really a game.

All twenty of the Brothers here stood ready to back his play and they had heard his declaration. By the rules of the Club all she had to do to make it official was to declare loyalty to the Club and they would be bound for life. That thought should have worried him but a not so small part of him hoped she would. They would find a way through this. If his President could claim an assassin as his Old Lady, he could find a way to make it work no matter what secrets Diana was hiding.

Hawk looked over at him with so many questions in his eyes it was hard not to look away. The gist of them all was… Are you sure? Highdive nodded. Relief filled him when Hawk nodded back.

Hawk looked over at Diana. "If someone who is family starts a fight, it is an internal matter. An Old Lady is loyal to the Club and we protect them. So they can't claim retribution for something they do as long as there is no permanent damage. He is asking if you are loyal to the Dark Sons and have bound yourself to Highdive for life."

Hawk's smile was challenging and Highdive knew there were volumes being said between the two of them. As soon as this confrontation was over he would demand to know how the two of them were connected. That just left protecting the girl. Maybe if she was Diana's sister they could get her covered under the same clause.

"Good to know. Of course I'm loyal to the Dark Sons." She said the words as if Tomasso was an idiot for asking.

"This is bullshit," Tony muttered. "We would have known if they were together. But that still leaves the Stepanov princess. She started this and I won't let her get out of her punishment."

The girl was a member of the Stepanov Bratva? That was going to make things exponentially harder. Was she related to Akula then? Realization hit him just as Diana raised her chin.

"So you think threatening to rape the President of the Dark Sons' daughter deserves no punishment?" She snorted. "That those tiny cuts on your face are going to be nearly enough for her father? And when her mother finds out," Diana let out a chuckle that was so cold it was as if the temperature dropped, "I think they are going to be finding your body pieces in interesting places for years."

Tony went white. "Akula is dead. She was killed four months ago."

"She was very much alive when I talked to her this morning." Diana shook her head as if pitying him.

Tomasso pinched the bridge of his nose and looked at Hawk. "You are telling me that your Enforcer's Old Lady is

Tishina, my father's favorite psychotic cleaner, and your daughter is the Princess of the Stepanov Bratva?" He shook his head. "Which would mean you slept with *Akula.* One of the craziest assassins in the world." He sighed. "You Dark Sons live dangerously."

Hawk was doing a good job of keeping a straight face, but Highdive could see the storm that was brewing beneath the surface. "Yeah. That is what I'm saying."

The girl in question gave a little wave. "Hey, Dad."

It was almost an hour before Highdive was able to pull Diana into his office for a much needed conversation. She had insisted on staying by the girl's side until all their visitors had left and Hawk had taken her back to his house for some much needed family time. Now that they were alone it was like the silence had grown thick between them.

Highdive's office was smaller than Hawk's because it was rarely used for meetings. He had a desk and chair and a small couch that he would catch naps on when things got tense and he didn't want to be bothered. The walls held framed photos from the different rallies he had gone to over the years as well as a few from his time in the Marines. The Dark Sons were his only family and he had just brought this woman, whom he cared for but barely knew, into the fold. He leaned back against his desk gripping the edge as he tried to corral his thoughts.

"Was anything you told me the truth?" They needed a reset before moving forward and he needed the full truth.

She sighed and shrugged out of her coat and placed it carefully over the arm of the couch. He was impressed, but not surprised, by the number of weapons that were revealed. Twin guns were holstered at her sides and blades were sheathed at her wrists. Hanging from her hip was a leather sheath filled with at least ten throwing darts. Another knife stuck out from the top of her right boot. He doubted those were all the weapons she had on her.

"I never lied to you."

He crossed his arms. "Is that so, Luna?"

She crossed her arms and stared back at him. "It's my name as much as Highdive is yours. Most people call me *Tishina*, I was born Diana, but I've been called many things."

She had a point though her name was the least of their worries. One of the biggest being did she feel even a small amount of what he did? But he wasn't ready to address that yet.

"What does *Tishina* mean?" It was very obviously a Russian word the way Diana said it. He knew that Akula meant shark but that was as far as his Russian went. Unlike many of his Brothers he hadn't learned multiple languages. He had focused his time on learning more physical things. He had mastered more martial arts than most people even realized existed.

"It means silence. My father called me his *smertel'naya tishina*, his deadly silence."

There was so much to unpack from that statement. What had it been like being raised by a man who would give such a nickname? He wasn't even sure where to start with his questions.

"You don't sound Russian."

She shrugged. "I wasn't allowed to talk much growing up. And I want nothing to do with that man or his family. I've gone to a lot of effort to make sure I sound nothing like him. When I'm around my sister it gets harder."

"Nadya? She's your sister?" He'd heard the girl's name before Hawk had taken her away but not a lot of detail. Though the girl hadn't sounded Russian either. Was she

Akula's daughter as well? He wasn't sure how old the woman was but that didn't seem possible.

"No, I'm sorry." She laughed, the sound lacking any mirth. "I don't know why I thought you would know. No one does. Nadya is my niece. Alena is my half-sister. She was the one shown off to guests. I was just the bastard's dirty secret." Bitterness was obvious in her tone.

"Do you still work for him?" He remembered Tomasso saying she was the Don's favorite cleaner. He doubted that she worked as a maid, so she must be a hired killer. It was odd because the Mafia and Bratva families rarely shared resources.

"No, not for a very long time. Most have forgotten that I was ever a part of the Bratva. I've worked as a freelance fixer for the last nine years."

Her voice was so dry and cold it reminded him of when they had first met at the club. It was her walls trying to keep him out as if she feared how he might respond to the new information. Fixers came in so many varieties from the barely legal to assassins who preferred a different occupation name. He was starting to get an idea that this woman was so much more complex than he had ever imagined.

"Why did you approach me at the club?"

"I told you why back then. Nothing has changed."

He remembered her words clearly. *I picked you because you are a focused, calculating, selfish perfectionist.* She claimed nothing had changed, but for him everything was different. He knew every inch of her body and could make her orgasm almost on command. Had been able to for over a month. Usually that was the point where he grew bored, but he had never even considered ending what they had.

He pushed off the desk and stalked over to her. She looked taller in her combat gear but the reality was she was small compared to him. Her chin was up as he stood in front of her but he could see her iron control slipping. He cupped her cheek and took in how beautiful she was.

"I was worried when you disappeared like that."

She blinked and her eyes softened. "I'm sorry I couldn't tell you more. I never lied to you. You may have assumed some things that I didn't correct, but I never lied."

Highdive shook his head and chuckled. "Like what?"

She smiled. "You assumed the men I told you about were ex-boyfriends. They weren't."

There had been a few nights when they had shared stories about awful dates and her lack of satisfaction from her partners. "If they weren't boyfriends, what were they?"

"Either marks I was getting information from or targets that I killed." Her muscles tensed under his hand as if she was readying herself for a blow.

Was that all she had ever known before? Not that he had ever gotten serious with a woman but there had been a few who had been more than a casual fling. How lonely must her life have been.

"Is that what I am? You never tried to get any information out of me. Do you plan on trying to kill me?"

"No! The truth is, being with you was the first selfish thing I'd ever done." She sighed. "I guess things have changed. If I was still the same woman as I was when we met I would have left you as soon as we started getting close. But talking with you, submitting to you, is one of the best decisions I've ever made."

"Why didn't you just tell me the truth?"

She pulled away from his touch and started pacing the small room. She was like a caged tiger, sleek and beautiful. "I thought about it. Several times. I almost did, but I was worried about how you would react. I didn't want to lose what we had." She stopped pacing and put her hands on her hips. She made quite a tempting picture with all the weapons and black clothing. "Besides, how do you even start that conversation? Hey, thanks for the fun time, by the way have I mentioned that I kill and steal things for money? Oh and you should know I've been stalking you and your club for months because my sister wanted to keep an eye on her husband. Hope you're not too mad and still want to tie me up and give me mind blowing orgasms."

Highdive laughed. He couldn't help it. The whole situation was ridiculous. For years he had harassed his Brothers telling them not to get mixed up with women because they were too complicated. Fate had a wicked sense of humor.

Diana scowled at him. "I'm glad I'm amusing you. I guess laughter is better than attacking me and forcing me to kill you."

Highdive strode over and she backed up until her back was against his bookshelf. Pressing his body against hers he leaned down and whispered into her ear, "I don't think you would kill me." He nipped her earlobe and enjoyed her shiver.

"I could." Her breathy response held little of the bravado she had been showing.

He ran his hands down her neck then across her shoulders slowly removing her shoulder holsters. She didn't fight him. Instead she stood still, her breath even. If it wasn't for her dilated pupils you would never know they were doing anything but having a pleasant chat.

He placed her rig on the chair next to them.

"I didn't say you couldn't, I said you wouldn't." He unbuckled her belt and slowly pulled it from the pant loops. The knife and dart sheaths slid off and he caught each one before they fell to the ground.

Diana swallowed. "I would have if you had attacked me. Most people don't take it well when they find out I'm an assassin."

He placed the weapons on the growing pile and got down

onto one knee. She was beautiful from this angle as well as every other one. Highdive removed the knife from her boot then ran his hands slowly up her legs. He found another gun and two more knives in his explorations and took those as well.

"Do you know what I was thinking when I saw you take down Tony?"

"No."

"I thought you were fucking gorgeous and sexy as hell. I was hard as a rock, even when you pointed his gun at me." He stood and added his newest finds to the collection.

"I don't think that is a normal reaction. Most men don't enjoy it when I point a gun at them."

Highdive stepped back and ran his hands up her sides. The stiff bumps he felt told him she had a concealed belly band under her shirt. This woman would never stop surprising him. He pulled her shirt off over her head then undid the Velcro that held multiple throwing knives. Her nipples were tight points against her bra and he brushed his fingers slowly around them.

"I never said I was normal." He tossed the band onto the chair and gripped the back of her neck taking her mouth in a brutal kiss.

For the first time since they had met at the Club she immediately met him with a fiery passion. She wrapped her arms around him and pressed her chest against his as if trying to get closer than their bodies would allow. It usually took edging her until she was mindless for her to react like this and he was surprised. Had she been holding herself back because they were in the Club or was it something else?

Highdive pulled back from the kiss and there was a wild light in Diana's eyes. They may have a lot of things to talk about, but that would have to wait. He needed to be inside her to reconnect with her and assure himself that this was real.

"Strip."

She smirked at his command. "Are you still trying to check me for weapons, or are we going to fuck?"

He loved this new aggressive side to Diana. He looked her up and down with a chuckle and stepped back.

"Why can't it be both?"

She laughed and with quick efficiency removed all of her clothes. He always loved seeing her naked. Her body was a lean, lithe example of what a woman should look like. She stepped forward with a seductive predatory grace that made his cock pulse inside his jeans. Her hands made quick work of his belt and zipper. He held back a groan as she reached inside and pulled him free.

Lightning sparked up his spine as she stroked him. Unable to wait any longer he took her mouth. They kissed like they were fighting. Their bodies slammed against the bookshelf and he couldn't care less about the items that he heard tumbling to the floor. Highdive picked her up so her legs wrapped around his waist without ever breaking their embrace.

He maneuvered himself until he was poised right at her entrance. Her wet heat felt like paradise against the tip of his cock as she tilted her hips. The warm embrace of her pussy felt like home as he slid into her depths.

Pulling back he then slammed forward and she threw her head back in a scream. He set a brutal rhythm that had them both panting until the shelf behind her crashed to the floor. Highdive stepped back knocking things off his desk and maneuvered them to the couch. He fell with her onto the leather surface driving deep inside her, never breaking their connection.

She contracted around him as the lamp fell to the floor shattering. The door burst open and he stilled, glaring at the intruders. Diana squirmed under him the movement squeezing his cock and almost pushing him over the edge of orgasm. He took a deep breath getting himself under control.

Sharp and Dragon stood in the doorway looking ready for a fight. Their expressions more shocked then could be accounted for on walking in on one of their Brother's fucking. He followed their line of sight and chuckled.

Somehow Diana had gotten a gun and was pointing it at his Brothers. His cock pulsed it's agreement with how sexy the sight of the woman under him was. Her finger wasn't on the trigger but he knew if it had been danger coming into the room they would have been dead.

"If you don't keep fucking me, I'm going to shoot you, and them." Diana's breathy growl broke the uncomfortable silence of the room as she lowered the gun so it wasn't pointing at anyone. But she didn't drop it completely.

His Brothers' laughter as they backed out of the room told him he was in for a rash of shit later. Highdive leaned in and kissed Diana's neck.

"Where did you even get that?"

She moaned and ground against him. He watched as she slipped the gun back into the pocket of her jacket that was on the arm of the couch they were using. Her ability to multitask was impressive. She clenched around him and all thoughts about weapons drifted away.

He thrust inside her and enjoyed the way she arched up to meet him. He had his marching orders and for once he didn't mind taking orders.

Chapter 8

Telling an angry woman to calm down works about as well as
baptizing a cat.

These were the moments that Diana had come to crave. When she sat wrapped in Highdive's arms and could relax. Sometimes they were silent, sometimes they talked about trivial things for hours. What they did didn't matter, what was important was the feeling of peace and safety that she found within his arms.

"You know, I'm never going to live that down." Highdive chuckled into her ear.

Diana snuggled against him, not caring that he was fully dressed and she was naked. She had never actually seen him naked. Though she loved when he took off his shirt. The tattoos spread across his broad muscles were gorgeous. Maybe now that they were doing things outside the Club she would get to see him in all his glory.

"Live what down?"

"The fact that you pulled a gun on my Brothers and threatened to shoot me if I didn't keep fucking you."

She chuckled. Men were so sensitive. "Oh that."

She played her fingers along the edge of his leather cut. Indulging in doubts or worry about the future wasn't something she usually did. But snuggled up against this man, she couldn't help but wonder what came next.

"Am I really your Old Lady now?"

He ran his hand down her hair. The gentle touch soothed something inside her. The commitment was important to him even if she didn't fully understand why. Their road might not be easy but she was willing to endure any hardship for him.

He kissed the top of her head. "Yes. Do you regret agreeing to it?"

Diana thought about it. While watching the Dark Sons for Alena she had done a lot of research on the men in the Club and on Outlaw Motorcycle Clubs in general. To them claiming a woman as your Old Lady was as good as a marriage. Hell, it seemed more logical than a traditional marriage that had over a fifty percent chance of failure.

The fighting exemption was a surprise, but it made sense. Was she ready to commit for life to this man? That he had been willing was shocking. The months they had spent together at Dark Secrets had been wonderful and intense but he hadn't even known who Diana really was.

Still, he hadn't hesitated when he thought she was in danger. The fact that he had been willing and actually wanted to claim her made her feel things she had never experienced before. Even if it had just been to save her meant more to her than he could possibly understand. Other than her sister, no one had ever chosen her. Or wanted to protect her.

People used her. She was valuable to them, not as a person, but only as a tool or a weapon.

"No. I don't regret it."

He gave her a gentle squeeze. "Good. Though I'm not sure I like how long you hesitated to say that."

"It's a lot to take in. Do you regret saying it?"

"No. We have a lot to work out. Things are dangerous right now. You'll have to stay here on the compound with the other Old Ladies and the kids until we deal with Petrov. But don't worry we'll keep you safe."

Diana sat up and scowled at him. She didn't like what he was implying. Staying on the compound had been her plan, but only in order to protect her niece. The way he was talking he thought he had the right to keep her locked up. That she needed him to keep her safe.

"I can take care of myself."

"I'm sure you can. But Diana, this is war." His soft look turned hard. "You and your niece will stay locked down in the compound until things are sorted. It's my job to keep everyone safe. Don't make that job harder by throwing a fit."

Don't throw a fit? All her good feelings brought on by the afterglow of sex popped like a bubble. Who the hell did he think he was talking to? He thought he was dealing with some over emotional girl? Diana stood, letting the calm she used when on a job fill her, and gave him cold eyes.

"You're going to keep us safe until you deal with Petrov? Fascinating." She raised an eyebrow. "How are you upgrading your patrols? Because I know your resources and they aren't enough to secure this entire property from what he has access to. Even if you do, how long can you maintain the heightened security? Do you even have a plan or rough timeline for taking down Petrov?"

Highdive sat up with a sigh that grated on her nerves. "That's Club business. All you need to do is follow instructions."

Diana crossed her arms, not happy with the brush off he was attempting to give her. His eyes locked on to her chest and heat flared in them for a moment. She snorted. Men were all the same, easily distracted, yet completely confident that they knew best. When he didn't add more to his comment she shook her head.

Words were not her weapon of choice and attacking him wouldn't help the situation, so she decided to remain silent. No one had had the right to dictate her life for many years and that was not going to change.

A shower to wash away the sweat from their exertions would be nice. Then she would begin her own plans. Diana slipped her clothes back on making sure her movements were slow and controlled. She needed the clarity that being in control always gave her if she was going to insure her niece was safe while being kept in the dark.

Highdive stood, walking over to her and bent to place a kiss on her neck. "There are going to be times when I can't tell you things, Diana. You have to trust me to know what I'm doing."

Diana didn't let him see her roll her eyes. Ignoring his words, she stepped out of his arms and quickly rearmed herself.

"What are you doing?" The frustration in Highdive's voice was evident, but she didn't care.

She walked around him and put her coat back on. Arguing at this point was stupid. She intended to stay, at least for now. If she thought Nadya was in danger or that some other action was needed then she would do as she always did and look out for her interests in whatever way was necessary. She pulled her car keys out of her pocket.

"You're not leaving." His command was a sharp growl.

Diana turned and stared at him. Would he actually try to stop her? It was tempting to put him in his place, but with deadly measures off the table her options were too limited.

The noise they made would attract his Brothers and that would end in things escalating out of control.

She was on a mission, the distraction of the last hour aside. She might care for this man more than she had ever cared for anyone other than her sister, but that didn't mean she would let him cage her like some delicate songbird. He could think he won for now, it would make doing what was necessary later easier.

She raised an eyebrow. "Don't throw a fit. Nadya and my bags are in the car. I'm going to go get them. Have someone tell me where we're going to be staying so I can take the bags there."

Suspicion was clear on his face. "I know you're mad, Diana. Don't do something stupid."

She crossed her arms and made a rolling, let's move this along, gesture with her hand. He growled and it was hard not to smirk. She had learned long ago how much people hated silence. They might say they hated arguing, but really, there was nothing more unnerving than a lack of resistance that you didn't trust.

"Fine, I have a house on the compound, but all the women are staying in the clubhouse tonight since the majority of the Brothers are going out on a run. That includes me and Hawk so the two of you will be here as well. I'll get one of the Prospects to find you two rooms."

She nodded and started out of the room.

"This is the way it has to be until things are safe," he shouted after her.

Diana didn't bother to look back.

The Dark Sons and their families were an interesting mix of people. It was one thing to read about them on paper while

observing them for her sister. Another to watch them inter-
acting with each other in this confined and stressful situation.
Diana had taken up a position near the back of the main
Clubhouse room at a small seating area behind the pool tables
where she could observe and not be in the way.

By her count there were about twenty non-combatants
among them who were being kept safe in the Clubhouse. Two
of those were infants and five kids under the age of thirteen.
Two of the men she had classified as non-combatants would
probably balk at the label, but she wouldn't count on the two
men in their late sixties to be of much help.

Two of the women seemed to be in charge of making
sure everyone had what they needed. Val, who was Dozer's
Old Lady, was a vibrant Southern Belle. She wandered
around talking to everyone with a baby on her hip. She
always had a smile and some sass for everyone she talked to.
Pixie, a small blonde woman who was Sharp's Old Lady,
seemed to be in charge of feeding everyone whether they
wanted it or not.

Diana shook her head. The gathering felt more like a
family reunion than a lockdown. Even Nadya had gotten into
the mood and was playing some sort of game with the kids
that seemed to be a mix of tag and tickle.

Brothers were constantly in and out of the offices in the
back hall. Fully armed and armored it was obvious they were
ready for some sort of action soon. Seeing men prepped for
battle wasn't unusual for Diana, what she couldn't wrap her
brain around was how gentle and caring they were with the
women and children. Never snapping at the kids who tried to
pull them into their games.

Although the mood was tense it wasn't hostile. No one
spoke directly to her, but they didn't seem to be hiding either.
Diana had managed to pick up bits and pieces of their conversations. Enough to figure out that the majority of the men

would be riding out soon on some sort of protection detail that was critical to taking down Petrov.

How many of them would be staying behind to protect the families? This building was secure with its concrete walls but it was large. Defending it against the kind of men the Russian could bring would be difficult.

If it had been up to her, she would have stationed at least two snipers on the roof. Then used another six men inside at strategic locations while keeping everyone not able to fight confined in the basement. Lastly, she would also arm the women as a final line of defense.

Not that anyone had wanted or asked for her opinion. Even when she'd tried to offer help the men had brushed her off. Even Hawk, who should know better, had dismissed her offer with a curt 'No'.

It was like they were so focused on a single plan that they couldn't even consider it might be flawed. Pride was the first of the deadly sins for a reason. She would have to keep her focus on protecting Nadya.

Highdive had attempted to talk with her several times. But he hadn't been interested in her opinions on defense. No, he had only wanted her to accept his weak platitudes. All the while telling her just to accept that Nadya would be safe and expecting her to agree to follow orders like a sheep. Diana had stopped listening to him once she realized his words were nothing but nonsense designed to make him feel better.

Asshole.

It was a petty pleasure but she enjoyed how obviously her one word answers frustrated him. She took perverse joy in watching him stumble for some new way to make her 'understand'.

Yes.

She understood that he had club business he couldn't talk about.

No.

She didn't plan on leaving.

Yes.

She was here to guard Nadya.

Fine.

They would talk later and work things out.

That last one she wanted to believe but wasn't sure it was possible.

The two of them were sexually compatible. Her body practically hummed any time he was near. If it was just chemistry, Diana could have walked away without a second glance. But some of her favorite memories of him had nothing to do with sex.

She cherished the hours they spent talking cuddled up on a couch after a scene at the club. She loved his mind almost as much as his body. It was amazing how much you could discuss without ever getting into personal history. They had covered topics ranging from philosophy to politics.

Unfortunately he didn't understand that those soft moments were a very small portion of who she was. He didn't seem to respect that the larger pieces of her personality made her a superior tactician and warrior. Oh he had said that seeing her take down Tony was erotic, but he didn't understand that that small confrontation was only a tiny glimpse into her skills.

Finding weak points and exploiting them in the most beneficial way was how she survived. Diana knew more about the Bratva than all of these men combined having grown up as one of them. Anything these Brothers thought they understood was secondhand knowledge at best. But because she was a woman, not a soldier they discounted her as weak.

Diana snorted.

Compared to the general population these men were elite.

They had survived boot camp and combat while surrounded and supported by their units. Still very few of them could match her skills when it came to killing. Her training under cruel taskmasters had started as soon as she could hold a blade. The people who had been responsible for raising her hadn't cared if she survived, only that if she did, she would be the deadliest of weapons.

She wouldn't accept being treated like a clueless child who needed to be protected.

It wasn't that she disagreed with the decision to leave her here while they went on the run. Most of the men didn't know her, and trust and teamwork would be critical if what they were doing was dangerous. But not making her part of the defense of the compound was foolish.

Hawk and Highdive knew her primary goal was protecting her niece. That she would do everything in her power to keep the girl safe. But they still lumped her in with the soft noncombatants. It was like buying an expensive security system but never arming it.

It was insulting.

People underestimating her wasn't unusual. It made her job easier and the targets easier to kill. Gaining Highdive's respect was important if they were going to be more than acquaintances.

Her pride demanded it. She couldn't be viewed as something weak and helpless. She wanted a partner. Her heart ached at the thought, but if she was going to stay things would have to change.

Diana shook her head, breaking off her circling thoughts. Cami approached her table. The beautiful curvy woman had purple hair that was a fascinating contrast to her pale skin. Married to Tek, one of the Dark Sons' officers, she was a highly skilled hacker with a moderate amount of self defense training. The pictures in Diana's file of her were odd. They consisted mostly of Cami dressed in a strange array of costumes.

Tonight the hacker was dressed almost normally in yoga pants and a large Dark Sons t-shirt. On her feet were a pair of neon pink combat boots. The woman's smile was a little too eager for Diana's tastes but that was probably her Russian upbringing.

"Hi! I'm Cami. I couldn't believe Tek when he t-told me Highdive had t-taken an Old Lady so I looked you up. *Tishina*, wow. That's some serious street cred you've g-got."

The woman's stutter was well known but Cami didn't appear embarrassed by it. Her reputation as a hacker must not have been exaggerated if she had dug up any information on her moniker *Tishina*.

Was she mocking her or really impressed? Hopefully neither.

"You can call me Diana."

Cami plopped herself down on the chair across from her. "So what's it like to b-be an assassin? I'm thinking it's not as glamorous as the m-movies say."

The woman's blunt question startled Diana. Most people only hinted around the edges of what she did for a living. If they had the nerve to even broach the subject it was with hesitation and disbelief. Honestly, people mostly avoided the topic unless they were trying to hire her.

Not that she talked to many people.

It was tempting to remain silent. Use her normal intimidation techniques to make the woman go away. But that wouldn't help her situation any. If she and Highdive were going to be together then it was probably a good idea to make nice with the other Old Ladies.

Diana shrugged. "It pays well, but the benefits suck."

Cami burst into laughter that was louder than the small

joke deserved. She slapped the table as if it was the funniest thing she had ever heard.

Was this woman mentally unstable?

A woman Diana didn't recognize joined them and looked at Cami with a shaking head. Long dark hair, the new woman was short with a gymnast's build. She stuck out her hand and ignored the cackling woman.

"Hi, I'm Jade. I'm Hannibal and Ink's Old Lady."

That those two men had claimed someone was a surprise. It must have happened while she was tracking down Alena. Diana shook Jade's hand and attempted a smile. "I met your men at Dark Secrets, they seem like good people."

Jade raised her eyebrows. "Oh, I didn't know you went to the… uhm… Club."

Was someone with two men embarrassed by the mention of a BDSM club?

Diana nodded. "That's where Highdive and I met. It's a nice place."

Jade bit her lip. "So you *met* Ink and Hannibal there as well?"

Cami stopped laughing and looked between the two of them with a worried expression. Why was she so concerned about where they had met?

Understanding dawned. The woman was jealous.

"I've never fucked your men."

"Oh good." Jade blushed then smiled nervously. "Now I won't have to try and kill you."

Diana laughed and leaned back. Did this woman realize how ridiculous her threat was? "Good to know."

Cami clapped her hands and gave a little squeal. "Dark Secrets, th-that's the BDSM Club, isn't it? Please tell me you t-tie up Highdive and make him kiss your boots. Because I will sooo hack their security feeds and get that footage."

Diana shook her head. Her man may had proven earlier

that he didn't always have to be in complete control but the idea of him kissing her feet in submission was ridiculous.

"No. Sorry to disappoint you."

"Well that is a bummer. T-Tek's not really into the formal BDSM scene. I've been trying to get him to take me to the Club for a wh-while but so far it's a no."

Jade rolled her eyes. "Like the two of you need a Club. You just start scening wherever you are."

"T-True, but I've heard they have some amazing equipment there," Cami whined.

"Like Tek wouldn't buy you whatever equipment you wanted to try out. Hell, you could buy it yourself if you wanted," Jade said.

"True."

Diana looked at Jade. "Will you be going to the Club with them now?"

The idea of being in a relationship with two men was strange to her. Having to deal with one was frustrating enough. But she was the last person to judge anyone on unusual partnerships.

Jade shook her head. "Unlike some people," she looked over at Cami with a smile, "I like to keep things a little more private. Not that there's anything wrong with the Club. I mean… no offense."

The woman looked horrified at the idea that she had just insulted her.

"No offense taken."

The silence stretched uncomfortably. Diana wasn't good at the whole making friends thing. What did someone say to normal women? Her usual conversation topics wouldn't work with these women. The only woman she talked to was her sister. They discussed weapons and a shared hatred of their family.

Diana's training wouldn't help either. Knowing how to

flatter men or deal with the lowest scum of the underworld wasn't the same as talking to regular people. Should she compliment their clothes?

Cami broke the silence. "So... you and Highdive. You k-kinda did things backwards."

"How do you mean?" Diana asked.

Jade shrugged. "I'm the newest Old Lady other than you. We all have pretty similar stories. We met one or more of the Brothers, got to know the Club. Received the 'what it means to be an Old Lady' speech from someone. Then get into some sort of trouble they have to save us from. Then become an Old Lady."

Were these women trying to say she didn't belong because she wasn't like them? It was amazing how casually they seemed to accept needing to be rescued. But that would never be her.

If Diana was honest with herself it wasn't the physical safety she longed for but the mental ability to not always have to be 'on'. Oh, it was nice knowing there was someone who could if necessary. But she wanted a partner who would watch her back. One that not only let her relax but forced her to.

"And until th-this one here." Cami jerked her thumb at Jade. "You fucked your man in front of at least five Br-Brothers."

Jade rolled her eyes. "Sorry if I broke the streak."

Exhibitionism wasn't her thing but it didn't worry her either. Diana and Highdive had had sex at the club multiple times and more than five people had been present so if that was a tradition it wouldn't be an issue.

"I'm sure at some point we'll have sex in front of the Brothers."

That was, if they were still together. Why did people get so uptight about sex? Highdive had shown her that with the right partner it was easy to forget you had an audience. Before him she hadn't enjoyed sex in private or public and had faked her way to the finish. Now that she knew what good sex was like she would miss it if he didn't pull his head out of his ass.

"Not the point." Jade cleared her throat as if trying to get Cami back on track.

What exactly were these women trying to tell her? Was this some sort of you don't belong here speech?

"Well, I can't go back in time and change things to suit your script." She gave them a cold expression. "I'm not the type of person who needs saving. More the type that people need to be saved from."

"Yeah your k-kill list is pretty impressive," Cami mumbled.

Diana sat back in her chair and glared at the two women. "Is that the problem? Most of your men's kill count is almost as high as mine. Do you have a problem because I did it for money or because I'm a woman?"

"No, not at all. Shit. We're messing this up." Jade made a frantic beckoning gesture towards someone.

Diana saw they were summoning Val, a vibrant red head who was the Old Lady of Dozer the Club's Treasurer. The woman smiled and handed her baby off to Tari, a tall beautiful African American woman before she headed their way.

Diana leaned forward. "What exactly are you messing up? If you don't want me in your little Club, have the backbone to say it straight."

Both of them looked at her with a mixture of embarrassment and frustration.

"What these lovely ladies were supposed to be doing was welcoming you to the fold. But by the hang-dog looks on their faces I'm guessing they might have fumbled that a bit." Val's southern twang was soothing though she looked at the two women like they were kids in need of a spanking. She was about the same age as Diana but where life had etched it's harsh marks onto the assassin it had softened and gentled Val.

Taking a deep breath Diana forced herself to relax. Keeping her temper under control shouldn't be this hard. Something about the idea of these women not accepting her had struck a deep chord within her. That on top of the stress caused by Highdive's dismissal had her off balance.

Why did it even matter to her? Alone most of her life she could easily continue down that path. Her dreams of settling down might be appealing, but they weren't set in stone. Even if her sister planned on trying to stay here with Hawk once the bloodshed was over, she didn't have to.

Diana had spent too much of her life surrounded by hostility. She wouldn't do that to herself again.

"Let's try this from the beginning." Val stuck out her hand. "Hi, I'm Val, Dozer's Old Lady. We'd love to get to know the woman who finally pinned down the grumpy, yet lovable Highdive."

Grumpy. She snorted. That was one word for the man.

"Diana."

"Now, Cami here has told us a lot about you and that has made some of the women too nervous to approach you. But I told them not to fuss so much. Highdive wouldn't choose someone who was dangerous to us to be his Old Lady."

Diana liked the friendly woman's blunt words. Depending on what information the nosey hacker had found out might not have painted the best picture. She forced a small smile onto her lips.

"Unless one of you has a contract out on you. You're safe from me."

Cami gave a nervous chuckle. "I usually have a f-few out on me but none that are in your p-price range."

Diana lowered her head and pinched the bridge of her nose. "Sorry, it was supposed to be a joke."

"How about we save all jokes involving killing till we know each other better?" Val patted her arm. "I'm not going to treat you like a country cousin and assume you don't know how things work in a Club. But much like our assumptions about you, I'm sure you have some about us. The most important thing you need to understand is that you're one of us now and those aren't just empty words. You and Nadya are part of our family and there isn't anything we wouldn't do for you. But that is only if you want to be here." She cocked her head. "Do you?"

Val's words hit a hollow spot in Diana's chest and made it ache. Her family for the most part was a disaster, her sister and niece being the sole exceptions. As a child she had dreamed about having a loving family. One that would care for her instead of use her like a disposable weapon.

Could she really risk believing in what this woman was offering?

She looked over at Nadya who was busy laughing with Pixie. This place was going to be her home. Nothing in life worth having was easy. Diana had conquered much harder challenges than making friends and making a pig-headed man see her worth. If she wanted even a chance at finding her place within this world it would have to start here.

"I think I do."

Her phone vibrated in her pocket. It surprised her because very few people had her direct number and she wasn't expecting her sister to call for several hours. Diana pulled it out and immediately recognized the number. She wished she could ignore the call and spend time getting to know these women. But that wasn't her reality.

"I'm sorry, ladies, I have to take this."

Diana strode away to try and find some privacy for her call.

Chapter 9

Don't try to cage a wild wolf unless you're hoping to have your
throat ripped out.

Highdive tried to focus on getting ready to ride. The
plan had been finalized and briefed, so there wasn't
much for him to do except keep people focused.
Taking possession of the truck full of body armor and
weapons from Minetti's men at the edge of their territory
should be quick and easy. They had done similar runs
hundreds of times but the stakes had never been this high.

Three weapons would be used to secure the loyalty of
their newer allies as well as expand the Dark Sons arsenal. If
Petrov attacked them directly every weapon and ally might be
needed. Tomasso Minetti was going to be at the pickup point
personally to share intel he hadn't wanted to disclose while
others were around.

It was crucial that nothing go wrong. He had hand chosen
the fifteen Brothers for the ride to ensure success. They were a

mix of officers and the most skilled fighters among them. Nothing short of a full-out assault could bring them down.

Having Diana here changed his focus making him doubt pulling all these people from the clubhouse. Were the compound defense strategies that had been in place for years sufficient? The men staying here were all good but the best shooters wouldn't be here. Should he have reworked the plan to compensate for that?

Highdive looked across the room. Hawk was calmly talking and joking with Dragon and Hannibal. How did that man never let the stress he was under show? To look at him you would never guess that he had just met the fully grown daughter he hadn't even known he had.

If he could function after getting that dropped on his lap, so could Highdive.

Hell, claiming an Old Lady and then fucking that up was barely even in the same league of stress. He needed to get his head on straight. Focus on what was needed in the moment. Later he could force his frustrating woman to say more than single word answers.

Grinder walked into the room from the kitchen and gave him a smirk. "Hey, Brother. Glad to see you're in one piece."

What the hell was his Brother talking about? Sharp chuckled from across the room and Highdive groaned.

Grinder gave him a fake concerned look. "I hope your lady respects your safe words. Remember, we're here for you if you ever need protection from her."

Highdive was going to beat the shit out of his friend if he kept this up. He'd known he was going to catch hell for the scene his Brothers had burst into earlier but had held out a little hope that they would forget it. Shaking his head he flipped off both of his chuckling Brothers.

"What the fuck are you guys talking about?" Hawk's deep voice cut through their laughter.

Grinder grinned. "We were coming down the hall earlier and heard what sounded like one hell of a fight. Shit crashing. Sounds of pain coming from Highdive's office. We thought the assassin had turned on him."

"That assassin is my Old Lady." Highdive growled.

Sharp chuckled and took up the story. "We burst through the door and before we can even figure out what's going on she's pointing a gun at us. Apparently we were interrupting their private time."

"She pointed a gun at you?" Hawk's tone was serious, but the side of his mouth ticked up in a small smile.

"Yeah," Grinder said. "First, she threatened to shoot us if we didn't leave and then to shoot Highdive if he stopped fucking her."

Hawk shook his head, amusement glinting in his eyes. "Sounds a lot like her sister. That whole family is crazy."

Highdive didn't want to talk about Diana. Especially since she was giving him the cold shoulder. So he tried to change the subject.

"How did your time with Nadya go?"

"She's apparently known all about me for years. It's hard not to be pissed at Alena but I don't have all the facts yet. For her to drop this on me in the middle of a goddamn war..." Hawk shook his head. "She has a lot to answer for."

Highdive could only imagine the stress his President was under. Protecting the Club. Wanting to kill the man who tried to kill him. Needing to protect his wife and child. Wanting to get to know his daughter.

With only half those problems Highdive felt the pressure frying his nerves. Was Hawk really taking this so well or was it a mask? He looked over at Diana and she gave him a cold stare.

"Trouble in paradise already?" Grinder asked.

"We're fine."

Hawk chuckled. "Took less ice than is in that glare to sink the Titanic, Brother. If you think that's good. You are so fucked."

Highdive took a deep breath. "She needs some time to get used to the way that we do things around here. I'm not even sure what she is mad about, but at least she seems to be listening and is willing to follow directions."

Hawk shook his head. "Yup, you're fucked. And not in the fun way. Your woman knows more about the dark side of life than most of our Brothers. Trying to treat her like the other women is going to blow up in your face."

"Oh, so you want me to invite her to Church? Find her a bike to ride out with us?" Highdive knew his tone was border-line disrespectful but he didn't like the implication that he should be putting Diana on the front line. Just the idea of purposefully putting her in danger turned his stomach.

Hawk leaned in, all humor gone from his face. "I think you need to take a breath, Brother."

Highdive did. He was out of line and he knew it.

Sharp cleared his throat. "I keep most shit from Pixie because she doesn't need it weighing her down. What you share or don't share with your woman is your business, but from what little I've heard, her kill count might be higher than mine. So treating her like she's naive might not be the best call."

Hawk nodded. "We've got a lot going on and none of us knows if this shit's gonna take days, weeks, or months to clean up. There are gonna be some hard choices that are going to have to be made but I don't want any of us forgetting why we are doing this." Hawk looked at each of them. "Family, not just Brotherhood. There is no reason to fight if we don't have something to fight for. Petrov needs to go down, but don't lose sight of why we are fighting."

Grinder nodded his agreement. Highdive was still trying to

process everything. He knew Diana wasn't weak but hearing that her kill count might be higher than a SEAL sniper was something he hadn't really thought about. He searched the room for her and saw her off to the side having what looked to be an intense conversation with Nadya.

He'd thought he knew everything he needed to know about her, but maybe he'd been wrong. The idea of her being a kick-ass assassin was hot as hell. It made her submission to him all the more precious. But could he deal with it outside the bedroom? Was he willing to treat her like one of his Brothers? He didn't like putting them in danger either but it never stopped him.

Nadya stormed off and headed towards the upstairs rooms. Diana shook her head and walked in their direction. Highdive took a moment to study her as she drew closer. The sense of hyper awareness that she always had at the Club now made sense.

It wasn't caused by past trauma, or at least not only by that. Her life was actually dangerous enough that she had to be ready to fight at a moment's notice.

No one should have to live like that. Soldiers on the front line burnt out because every moment of every day was dangerous. How had she not snapped?

Maybe he could show her that she could be safe with him. That she could let go of the tension that kept her muscles strung so tight and live a more normal life.

"Hawk." Diana's voice was filled with tension. She didn't even glance at him. Highdive knew in that moment that he had fucked up more than he imagined. "I received a call from a contact that says he has info on Petrov. I'm going to drive out to meet him. Can you put an extra guard on Nadya until I get back?"

She wanted to leave the safety of the clubhouse? He didn't

have enough men to send someone with her. There was no way.

"We're under lockdown. You can't leave." Maybe not the best choice of words but Highdive didn't take them back.

Her glare would have slit his throat if it had been a physical thing. Hawk for his part stayed silent which Highdive appreciated. Grinder and Sharp stepped away obviously not intending to get in the middle of what was probably going to be a bad argument.

Seconds passed and he waited for Diana to lose her temper, but she just looked between the two of them. Her silence was almost worse than fighting. He would not back down. The safety of everyone was his responsibility, she would just have to accept that.

Her voice when it came was razor sharp ice. "Hawk, would you give me a moment with Highdive."

Hawk nodded. "Whatever he decides I'll back. That's the way it works, Diana."

"Let's both hope he chooses wisely then." Her words sent a chill down his spine.

The two of them stepped away and Highdive racked his brain for the right things to say. They only had a short amount of time before the Brothers had to ride out and he needed her safe here so he could focus on the mission. He hoped explaining his reasoning would help calm her down.

"I'll take you to talk to your contact tomorrow. I can't spare someone to go with you tonight."

Diana's dry chuckle told him his placating words did not have their desired effect.

"My contact will only meet with me alone and only tonight."

"No, it is too risky. It could be a trap."

"I think it's adorable that you think you can say 'No' and I'll just listen. Do you think you can stop me?"

"I won't be able to focus unless I know you are safe. You will stay here."

"That sounds like a *you* problem. I am going."

Anger at her attitude had him speaking before he really considered. "I have forty armed Brothers here. So I think you will be staying here."

"Really?" Her voice was like warm silk as she moved closer. All his nerves fired as if he had stepped on a landmine. "I'm going to give you three scenarios to choose from and I suggest you choose wisely. First, you'll be smart and say *Diana, stay safe* and I go meet my contact. When you're back from your super secret mission I'll let you know what he said." She stepped forward and ran her hands down his chest. It was a sensual move and didn't match what she was saying. "Second scenario, I pretend to comply and as soon as you let your guard down I take out anyone in my way and Nadya and I disappear until this war is over."

Highdive felt the prick of steel against his thigh and realized she had a blade pressed against his femoral artery. He shouldn't find the situation arousing but apparently his dick disagreed because it was rock hard and pressing painfully against his zipper. He cleared his throat.

"And the third option?"

"You try to have your Brothers disarm me now so you can *talk sense* into me when you get back."

He winced, since that was exactly what he had been thinking of doing. She was an impressive woman who had apparently thought this through.

"What would you do then?"

She chuckled and backed him against a wall. They were now shielded from view. It took a moment for Highdive to realize she had maneuvered them so that to everyone else it looked like they were having an intimate moment. She leaned in and whispered into his ear.

"I'll let you in on the biggest difference between soldiers and assassins. Soldiers are trained to hesitate before killing. By the time they determined I was a threat several people would be dead and I'd already be out the door. Nadya would have climbed out the window like instructed. I give myself a 70% chance of getting away without anything more than minor injuries."

His mind spun trying to adapt to the new reality that he found himself in. Was she really as dangerous as everyone claimed? And was he willing to risk it to keep her away from possible danger?

"You'd kill someone for trying to keep you safe?" He was both horrified and fascinated by her words.

Diana didn't flinch. Resolve was in every inch of her body when she said, "There are less than a handful of people I would hesitate to kill when it comes to my freedom or the safety of my niece." She sighed. "I don't need someone to protect me, Highdive. I care for you more than I thought possible, but I will never let someone hold me prisoner again for any reason. Please don't make me choose between hurting the people you care for and doing what I know is necessary."

"Who is this contact that is so important?" Highdive growled. He had little choice but to let her go but it was a bitter pill to swallow.

She reached up and cupped his cheek. The chemistry between them flared like a heatwave and it took all his willpower not to kiss her. It was messed up and unhealthy but even with the threats and anger he was still drawn to this woman.

"I can't tell you." Diana smiled and a small amount of warmth returned to her eyes. "It's safer for both of us if you don't know."

Highdive couldn't help but chuckle. How many times had he said those words to people? He didn't like being on the other end of the conversation. He leaned down and pressed his forehead to hers.

Though every cell in his body protested, he knew there was no way to make her stay now and not lose her in the long term. They had so much to work out between them but time and circumstances meant those discussions had to wait. He inhaled trying to memorize her scent.

"Stay safe, Diana. We have a lot to discuss when you get back."

Chapter 10

Tell your father that hovering is something that should only be done by helicopters.

How dare he try and stop her from going to this meeting?

Diana gripped the steering wheel breathing deeply. Highdive was just lucky she understood the fragile egos that men had or she would have demonstrated just how much she didn't need his protection. From day one she had made it very clear to Highdive that she would not give up control outside of the bedroom.

Did he respect that? No! Instead, the very first time they were together outside of the club he tried to assert his *manly alphaness* and stop her from doing what was necessary. She wouldn't try to tell him how to do his job. Why couldn't he have given her the same respect?

A small rustle of movement from the floor in her back seat had her rolling her eyes. Now wasn't the time to be distracted.

She needed to text someone that Nadya was safe with her before people panicked.

Who should she let know about her unexpected passenger? She had contact numbers for several people in the club. Settling on the one least likely to piss her off she fired off a quick message.

Diana: *This is Diana. Don't know if the men have noticed but my niece is no longer on property.*

Val: *That girl is going to be in more trouble than a lobster in a steel pot. Yes, they've noticed. I reckon she's with you?*

Diana: *Yes. I'll keep her safe and bring her back later.*

Ignoring the multitude of texts that soon scrolled across her screen, she locked the phone, and focused on driving. If her phone hadn't been on silent her niece would have been tipped off that something was up. As it was Diana was insulted that the girl thought a blanket was enough to hide her curled up on the floor.

She had considered sending her back immediately before leaving the compound but had changed her mind when she saw only one sniper on the roof. The girl would be safe with her. Once this mission was over a lesson in stealth and concealment was obviously needed. For now the girl could stay ignorant of her failure hiding in the very uncomfortable small space on the floor.

The back roads of Colorado were deserted and lit only by the night sky. Diana had no trouble finding the location of her meeting since she had been there several times before. Over the last few years it felt like the Denver area was a second home to her place in NYC. Watching the Dark Sons had only been the most recent of the many jobs she'd done in this beautiful state.

The wooded area screened a small ridge that was also a convenient sniper perch near one of the Mafia's favorite drop points. She had acted as a silent guardian for many exchanges over the years. Not that Tomasso or any of his men knew that. Donavan Minetti, his father, liked to have extra insurance over his son's safety.

She thought it was cute. Hiring an assassin to watch over your heir. Like a criminal version of a helicopter parent.

The overprotective dad himself stood next to a black BMW as if stargazing into the quiet night. Two of his men sat in the front of the car and didn't look like they were happy about it.

She knew Donavan often refused his bodyguards' requests to stay safely under their watch, making their jobs harder. Still deadly in his own right, he wasn't someone who hid behind others. Much to the frustration of his bodyguards, they often met without anyone else around to keep what they discussed private.

In his mid-sixties, Donavan hadn't allowed himself to fall out of shape like many of his contemporaries. His lean build spoke of health and vitality. The man had maintained the position as Don of one of the most powerful families by being smarter and more brutal than any of his rivals. Diana respected him not only because he paid well and stayed loyal, but because he honestly cared about not only his son but his daughter who had chosen to leave the family business.

She turned off the car and got out. Donavan opened his arms in greeting as she walked towards him. As always his words were warm and welcoming and flavored with a light Italian accent.

"Tishina so good to see you well."

She stepped into his embrace, as was their custom, though she still didn't understand why he always hugged her. It made both of them vulnerable. He treated her almost like she was family rather than the bastard daughter of one of his rivals. She kissed his cheeks in the ritualistic way he preferred to show affection.

"Always good to see you, Don Minetti. Though I am surprised to be meeting you in person."

Chuckling he stepped back, freeing her from his embrace. He waved off her words with a dramatic gesture. "You are mistaken. I am not here. I am happily vacationing in the Hamptons while my son proves himself with this nasty business."

She shook her head. "Of course you are."

He glanced over her shoulder and raised an eyebrow. The Don dramatically whispered, "Did you know you have a stowaway?"

Diana rolled her eyes and lowered her voice. "My niece thinks she is stealthy. I'm pretending not to notice till we finish talking or she would try to be out here *helping*."

They walked away from the cars and listening ears, up the hill and through the trees. When they reached the ridge they stopped. Down below a truck with its headlights on was parked along with two SUVs. Diana got a sinking feeling in her stomach. The two of them stayed back in the shadow of the woods so that no one below would be able to see them.

"That business with her Grandfather was shameful. Children should not be treated like currency to be traded."

"I agree though many would not."

"A man weak enough to need to trade family for power doesn't deserve respect. Was that your work at the Carolina house and cabin upstate? From what I heard it was messier than your usual style."

Normally she wouldn't share information like that with anyone, but this man had become the closest thing she had to a real father. They shared many secrets that would go no further than the two of them.

"Some. But mostly Akula."

"Then she is still alive? Good. How is she doing? Is she planning to replace your father?"

That would be a complete disaster. Diana loved her sister but the woman was ruled by her emotions. Chaos often followed her wherever she went. The two of them might be equally deadly but where she paused to look her sister leaped blindly.

"No. She is currently working on securing her retirement." That was a polite way to describe hunting down and killing anyone, including their father, who might be a danger to her. "Neither of us are interested in trying to save that particular ship."

"Good. Things will settle back down soon then?"

Diana knew what he was asking. With her father gone, the Russians would lose much of their influence in NYC. Other families would try to step up, but the Italians would easily maintain control of the lion's share of the businesses. If her sister took over it would most likely mean war, not only here, but back there.

"Yes. At least as far as we're concerned."

"We're?" Donavan looked surprised and disappointed. "Are you retiring as well?"

Diana hesitated.

Was she?

Could she be happy settling down? Stepping away from the danger and chaos should sound appealing. But Diana enjoyed her job. It held challenges that couldn't be found anywhere else. Ways to push herself both mentally and physi-cally. What would she do if she retired?

Money wasn't an issue. But she couldn't see herself living a quiet life. Not yet. But maybe she could slow down. Only take the jobs that interested her.

"I don't think so. But maybe I'll scale back. Take more time with family."

He laughed. "Good for you. But you will give me warning if I need to find a replacement, right?"

"I will." She nodded. "Now why are we meeting out here in the cold night air?"

"I have a job for you."

"I thought you said you had information?"

"It is a bit of both." The Don sighed. "You know me. I try to let my son stand on his own. So that he can learn and grow. Someday take my place."

Diana snorted. The man was very good at *the appearance* of letting his son stand on his own without actually doing it. "Of course. But you said on the phone this had to do with Petrov. Is your son changing sides?"

What would she do if he was?

Turning on the Dark Sons and by association her sister wasn't an option. The thought of betraying Highdive churned her stomach. No, she had given her word and even for this man she wouldn't betray them. But she also didn't want to burn this relationship.

"No. But as are many of the young, he is too trusting. His childhood friendship blinds him to the snake in his midst."

Only one man was considered Tomasso's childhood friend. The same man who was the reason she never worked directly for the Don's son. Tony. It wasn't a surprise that the man would try to partner with someone like Andrey Petrov. It was shocking that he would turn on Tomasso. Only a fool would willingly get on Don Minetti's bad side. His anger and vengeance would be biblical in response.

"You're sure? You know I have no love for Tony, but I never thought him dumb enough to cross you."

"He has a *brilliant* plan to frame the Dark Sons for my son's death. All while stealing millions. He even has a not so secret tropical paradise arranged to escape to if he thinks I've figured him out."

That did sound like Tony. The man believed he was better, smarter than everyone around him.

"Why are you telling me and not Tomasso?"

Donavan sighed. "Because if I show my son the proof he will get angry because I don't trust him and have been spying on him and his men. If I don't, and just stop it from happening my son will hate me for killing his friend. I've warned Tomasso for years that that bastardo is nothing but an anchor around his neck. But does he listen? No."

Trust was an odd thing. In Tomasso's place she would have assumed the Don was watching and had plants within his closest associates. But for some reason others considered that too controlling.

What would it be like to have someone care about her like that? She shook her head. Didn't she already have someone like that in her life?

Highdive would do that and more to try and keep her safe. It was literally what he did for the Club. His trying to stop her from going out alone was a perfect example of his protective nature. Maybe she needed to consider forgiving him for being high handed. Not that she would let him dictate her actions, but she could be understanding of why he tried.

"What's the plan? You give me the proof and I take the blame for spying on his men?"

It wasn't a bad plan but depending on the quality of the evidence Tomasso might not believe her. The hostility between her and Tony would cloud the issue.

"No. It is time for my son to learn a lesson the hard way. He must feel the knife in his back so he won't make this mistake again."

"What is the plan then?" Diana had the feeling she really wasn't going to like what the Don intended.

"First, I need you to agree to the job. I will give you every-thing I have on Tony and Andrey Petrov but only if you agree to do this my way." Steely determination filled Donavan's words. Arguing with him would be pointless. He wasn't the friendly man who gave hugs anymore. This was the ruthless Don who ruled his empire with a bloody grip.

"I'm listening."

"You will kill Tony, but only after my son knows fear. He must see with his own eyes that he has been betrayed. He must learn that he has been blind and enemies can smile while standing by your side."

Diana didn't like the picture he was painting. She avoided taking risks like that. Preferred a clean kill when the target was unaware.

"If I wait, your son could be hurt or killed. Are you really willing to risk that?"

Pain flashed across his face but was quickly replaced with resignation.

"Tomasso chose to be part of this life. He wants to lead the family some day. I've foolishly sheltered him hoping he would change his mind." He sighed. "He is too soft. I won't always have someone there to protect him. I should leave him to face this on his own with only the people he has chosen at his side. It's what my father did, but I can't. I need to know he has some chance of surviving."

"And if Tomasso dies?"

"I won't blame you."

She had her doubts that it would be that simple. It would be better to just take Tomasso's anger than risk the Don's grief. But that wasn't an option. She wouldn't break her word if she gave it.

"I don't like this."

"Will you take the job?"

"Do you have a plan to put me in the right place at the right time?"

"I do. But I'll only share those details if you agree to wait to act until my son's life is in imminent danger."

This was not a good idea. Under normal circumstances

she would never agree to a job blind like this. Her gut told her that if she refused not only would Donavan be mad but she would lose the Minetti's support for the Dark Sons against Petrov.

"Time is running out, Tishina."

She growled her agreement. "I will hold off if I can, but it will be my call."

He gestured to the clearing. "Down below thirty of Petrovs men are waiting to ambush my son and the Dark Sons in about fifteen minutes."

"And you want me to let them?" Anger at the last minute notice had her throat tightening. She was a planner and fifteen minutes was not enough time.

"That is the deal. Tony plans on drawing them all in before the double-cross."

"What the hell am I supposed to do against thirty hostiles?"

She was good but those odds were impossible without a lot more preparation. The sounds of vehicles echoed in the night and she cursed, sprinting towards her car.

"I'll transfer the information to our usual drop box. Good luck."

She popped open her trunk and pulled up the false floor. Her entire portable arsenal including several very illegal high-powered weapons were neatly laid out before her. She grabbed her favorite sniper rifle and the ammunition bag. Knowing she needed to get set up quickly if she was going to be able to do anything to help Highdive and his Brothers.

She cursed in Russian. It would take time she didn't have to locate all the enemies. Minetti's car started and she wanted to scream. Two more guns would be helpful but that would expose Donavan for the meddling father he was.

Fuck!

"Aunt Diana what's wrong?"

How could she have forgotten Nadya was in the back of her car? Taking a deep breath Diana called on her training and sank into the calm she would need to make it through the next hour.

"Grab the spotters scope, choose some weapons and ammo and meet me up there. You will follow my directions exactly or I will hog-tie you until this is over. Am I clear?"

"Y-Yes." All color had drained from Nadya's face. "But what's going on?"

"We're about to find out if you can put your training to good use."

Chapter 11

Never look a gift RPG in the muzzle.

The day had been nothing but one giant SNAFU and it wasn't over yet. Tomasso Minetti had changed the meet up location at the last minute which meant they weren't able to scout the location. Instead of having snipers positioned for backup and well laid out contingency plans they were going in blind with a hastily thrown together strategy if things went sideways.

In the middle of planning they had realized Nadya couldn't be found, costing them precious time looking for her. Hawk was in a volatile mood and wasn't pleased to find out she had stowed away with Diana instead of staying home safe. Highdive was on edge as well not knowing what kind of situation the two women were in.

He hadn't felt this out of control since he'd been a raw recruit. This mission was important but did the benefits outweigh the risks they were taking? Every fiber of Highdive's body said the smart move was to call this drop off, but he had been overruled.

Hawk didn't want them hamstringed by the blowback of not getting the promised equipment if Petrov attacked. It would be days, if not weeks, before they could reschedule and that would only be if Minetti didn't call off the whole thing. Their intel said the Russian was moving on them sooner rather than later.

The new location was perfect for privacy but it sucked for security. Well off the main roads and miles from any houses, but it had too many vulnerabilities. Which was why they had originally gone with the other location. Just the thought of the large clearing in the middle of nowhere surrounded by woods caused the strategic side of him to twitch. Hell, there were small cliffs on one side that could hide a hundred snipers.

The best plan he could come up with was to keep ten of the Brothers mobile on their bikes, while Tek and a few others rode in a van using their high-tech shit to try and spot danger. They had two drones they could launch if necessary, but there was only so much technology could compensate for. They needed to make this quick. Take possession of the truck and get the fuck out of Dodge.

The hairs on the back of Highdive's neck rose almost painfully as they rode down the dirt road towards their destination. The truck they would be picking up was just visible in the distance.

His shoulders were as tight as steel. Was it just the stress of everything or was there something wrong? Fuck it. He hadn't survived this long by ignoring his instincts.

Highdive keyed the mic to the earpieces they were all wearing. "I don't like this. Sharp, Rooster and Grinder peel off, stay back and watch our backs."

Hawk nodded and the three men in question slowed then turned around once the rest of them had passed. A small amount of the tension weighing down his shoulders lifted knowing they would have the extra eyes and guns at their backs. If only they could have gotten Sharp here and set up as overwatch earlier.

Scanning the woods and clearing ahead Highdive didn't see anything out of place. Minetti had two SUVs parked near the truck and five men stationed around the area. They were relaxed, barely even reacting as the Dark Sons seven bikes and Teks' van pulled up. The Italians had the headlights of the vehicles all on which made for easy visibility on the field but killed any possibility of seeing into the surrounding forest.

Tomasso and Tony looked like they were having a heated discussion as they stood by the side of the truck. From what Highdive knew those two had been inseparable since childhood. What could have them at odds?

Hawk gave the signal and Tek pulled around next to the truck. Three Brothers parked their bikes near the SUVs and two circled around to the back of the truck to take up positions.

That left him and Hawk to pull up in front of Minetti. Tomasso looked pissed as he waited for them to approach while Tony looked eager. The man was practically vibrating with a sick kind of glee that had Highdive itching to pull his weapon.

Tomasso gave Hawk a tight smile. "Sorry for the last minute change. Since you insisted at the last minute that I be here Tony thought more discretion was needed so that Petrov couldn't set anything up."

What the hell was he talking about? Tony had been the one who had said after the meeting earlier that Tomasso wanted to meet Hawk. The only last minute changes had been on the Italians' side.

Hawk's eyes narrowed. "That is not how we do business. I didn't ask for you to be here. All we want is the truck. It was your man who said you had intel you wouldn't share until now."

Tomasso looked confused and cold started seeping into Highdive's gut. "Which one of my men? I never said I wanted to meet personally."

The sound of a round being chambered ended the mystery. Tony pressed a gun to the side of Tomasso's head. Movement at the tree line quickly followed. It was hard to get a good count but if Highdive had to guess there were over twenty men now surrounding them with assault rifles.

Options and tactics raced through his mind. Three of them were outside the killing zone but that wouldn't be enough to save everyone. The trucks could be used as cover and they had on body armor but since most of his Brothers were only armed with handguns it would be a bloody fight.

"Tony?" Tomasso managed to put a world of anger and confusion into that name.

"Everyone keep your hands off your weapons or my men out there will start killing to make a point," Tony shouted.

Sharp's whispered voice came over their earpieces. "We've got at least thirty hostiles in play. Grinder and Rooster are circling on foot to see if there are any more hidden and provide support if needed. I'm going to see if I can get to high ground."

Highdive wasn't sure how much help they would be able to give but prayed their haste in coming here tonight wouldn't cost lives.

"You're going to kill us all anyway. Not much incentive not to take you out as well." Hawk's voice was calm.

"What the hell do you hope to accomplish with this, Tony?" Tomasso asked.

"I bring you and the thug to Petrov and I get enough money to keep me in luxury for the rest of my life somewhere your father will never find me. If you both come nicely I'll even let all your men live."

Did the man think they were idiots? There was no way they would let them live. Petrov would kill Hawk and use Tomasso as a hostage right up until the moment he realized his father wouldn't be blackmailed.

Donavan Minetti was a cold bastard that was known to take more comfort in bloody vengeance than the peaceful return of a hostage. Highdive met Hawk's gaze and saw the same knowledge in his eyes. His President gave the hand signal to hold.

"There is nowhere on this planet I won't find you. You were my brother and you threw it away for money?" Tomasso spit.

Tony grabbed Minetti's arm and pulled him towards the front of the truck while he ranted. "I was never your brother. Your father treated me like I was your lapdog, not family." Hawk gave the signal to ready. The two men were so caught up in their argument they were unaware of anything else.

Tomasso pulled his arm out of Tony's grip as they got to the hood of the truck. "You're right. A brother wouldn't betray me like this. My father warned me not to trust you. That you had greed and jealousy in your heart. I thought he was being a paranoid fool. But he was right, you are nothing but a coward."

The men from the forest were slowly closing in. Highdive knew Hawk would have to give the signal to act soon if they wanted any hope of being able to take cover and fight back.

Tony raised his gun and pointed it at Tomasso's head. "Maybe I'll just kill you and tell your father Hawk turned on us."

Tony's head exploded in a fountain of blood and brains followed by the distinctive echo of a high-powered rifle. For a single heartbeat the world seemed to pause before the sound of a second shot kicked everything into high gear.

Highdive grabbed Tomasso and dragged him after Hawk towards the cover between Tek's van and the truck carrying the weapons they could really use right now. Bullets flew through the night pinging off the vehicles.

Two of the enemies close to them crumpled to the ground like puppets with their strings cut. Whoever the hidden sniper was, they were on the Dark Sons' side.

"Nice shooting, Sharp," Hawk's voice came over the coms. "I need a sitrep."

"Sniper's not me. I'm heading to the ridge where the shots are coming from." Sharp's voice was tight.

Teks voice cut in, "Five men have Hannibal and Ink pinned down behind their bikes. Going to take Smoke and see if we can break them—"

An explosion behind the truck rocked all of them with its shockwave.

Highdive looked over at Hawk. "Did Ink bring grenades?"

"I think we have two friendlies on the ridge and one of them has a fucking RPG." Tek's voice was tight. "I'm sending a drone that way to see if we can get an ID."

Highdive cursed the decision not to have them already in the air before they arrived. So many bad calls had been made because they didn't want to anger Minetti and screw up the deal. He would never again back down on the things he considered necessary for safety.

"Are those your men on the ridge?" Hawk asked Tomasso.

Stepping around the two men, Highdive maneuvered to look past the end of the truck without losing the cover of the van. Ink and Hannibal were sprinting towards them. Of the five hostiles that had been pinning his two Brothers down three were down but two were scrambling to get back to their feet. Highdive fired several rounds into each of those men.

"Not that I know of," Tomasso answered as Hannibal and Ink joined them in the cover the van provided.

Hannibal looked pissed but unhurt. The large sniper from Louisiana didn't often lose his cool but when he did it was intimidating. "I haven't seen a rocket explode that close since the sandpit. Who the hell brought the heavy artillery?"

"No clue," Hawk replied.

Ink gave his friend a slap on the back. "Don't look a gift RPG in its muzzle. Let's be happy the man with the rockets is on our side."

Another explosion sounded from the other side of the field and they were all drawn into the firefight. Hawk got the side door of the van open and handed Highdive a TAR-21 assault rifle. The men attacking might have had the element of surprise but now that it was gone, it was obvious they didn't have training.

The sniper was still in play as Highdive saw several more people drop. A rocket fired past their location into the trees and from the screams it was obvious some of their attackers had been hiding in the cover.

"Shit, someone took out the drone," Tek's voice was annoyed.

Less than a minute later the silence of the night pressed in on him and Highdive realized it was over. Slowly he stepped out of cover and took in the scene. Over twenty men lay dead scattered around the field like discarded toys. His pulse was racing as he tried to make out if any of them were his Brothers.

"Everyone check in," Hawk barked over the comms.

Slowly Highdive relaxed as reports came in from everyone they had brought in. There were minor injuries but nothing critical. They had five prisoners and Minetti had lost three of the men who had been by the SUVs.

Sharp's voice came over their coms, "I've got eyes on our backup on the ridge."

Why did he sound so amused?

"Who is it?" Hawk growled.

"Your daughter and Highdive's woman. You all might want to get your asses up here."

Chapter 12

Before you accept a helping hand you should check to see if it's holding a knife.

"**O**f all the weapons you could have chosen. Of course you pick the RPG-7."

Diana looked back at her niece with a shake of her head. Did no one in her family appreciate the elegance of precision over chaos? Everyday it became more and more obvious how much the girl was like her mother. During the firefight instead of quiet deadly professionalism the cursing bundle of energy was borderline distracting.

Like mother, like daughter.

Diana smiled and swept her scope over the field below in a final check before packing up. Twenty three prone bodies. Five kneeling prisoners. Fourteen live friendlies. Nothing more for her to do and their time on the high ground was running out.

A few minutes ago she had watched Sharp break off from the main group heading towards the trail that led up to their ridge. The path he had taken snaked through the forest but the former SEAL wouldn't find it a challenge and would be reaching them any minute.

Nadya snorted. "With those numbers, it seemed like distraction would be useful."

"You had no idea of the numbers when you grabbed the launcher from my trunk."

Her niece bit her lip and seemed to lose some of her light. "Did I screw things up?"

Diana let out a slow breath remembering that Nadya was young and still needed encouragement. "No. You did well." But was it luck or skill? "Where did you learn how to fire it?"

Launching a rocket from the shoulder mounted device wasn't hard, but accuracy with one wasn't common, even in the military. Besides being illegal the rockets were expensive and hard to come by. Even though they were a significant distance away and tightly grouped, her niece had managed not to hit anyone on their side of the conflict.

"Mom likes exciting vacations."

Diana laughed, not doubting that for a moment. Nadya relaxed and practically vibrated with excitement as she started telling her about the last time she had gone on vacation with her mother. The unused adrenaline had the girl bouncing like a small child.

Movement in the trees to their right. Diana rolled to the left and palmed her Glock. It was probably Sharp, but it never hurt to be prepared.

A muffled voice was barely discernible over her niece's excited words but Diana thought she heard the man say, "Get your asses up here."

She called out loudly, "Be useful instead of creepy and help us carry this stuff back to my car."

Nadya stopped her bouncing and squinted into the darkness. Sharp stepped out of the woods and Diana holstered her gun. The man looked equal parts confused and amused to see the two of them.

Explaining how the two of them ended up acting as backup for the exchange was going to be complicated without sharing secrets. Diana didn't want to have to do it twice, so she bent to gather up her gear. Telling an edited version of that story could wait until whoever he had called joined them.

"Yes, ma'am." Sharp shook his head and chuckled.

Between the three of them they quickly transported the pile of weapons back down to her car. Most of the hardware hadn't been used but over-prepared was better than under. Tension roiled through Diana's stomach. Even with all her weapons she almost hadn't been enough to save Highdive.

The headlights of the cars and motorcycles had spot-lighted the combat like a badly directed movie. With planning the two to one odds wouldn't have been unmanageable, but Tony's unexpected betrayal had given the enemy the element of surprise. It was a miracle things hadn't gone a lot worse.

Thankfully, Tony was an awful tactician. Had she planned the ambush the Dark Sons wouldn't have had time to react. The attackers would have opened fire from cover. Hostages were a waste of time when it was obvious that survivors would be a liability.

Fortunately, Tony thrived on drama instead of practicality. Well, there was nothing more dramatic than a well-timed head shot. Diana smiled even as chills of fear raced across her skin.

If Tony had acted even a minute earlier, Highdive would have died. She'd barely gotten her rifle assembled when every-thing went pear shaped. If Tony hadn't been unreachable behind the cab of the truck she would have ignored her promise to Dominic Minetti.

Waiting for the pompous Italian to finish his speech and move from behind the cover had required every last ounce of her patience. During those long seconds so many possibilities had raced through her mind. Tomasso dead. Hawk dead. Highdive dead. The fact that her vengeance would have been bloody wouldn't have made a bit of difference.

When the men came out from the trees with their guns pointed towards Highdive she'd almost thrown away all of her training and changed priorities.

The effective use of the RPG-7 had saved most of the Dark Sons. Diana wouldn't have even considered using it the way her niece had. But without the large explosive damage and distraction the night could have turned out very different.

Diana tried not to smile as she listened to Nadya brag to Sharp about her part in the battle. The girl sounded more like a kid describing a cool scene from a video game than a young woman who was responsible for at least five deaths that night.

Diana's own kill count had increased by seven, not that she bothered to track the total any longer. The Dark Sons and maybe Tomasso's men had been responsible for the other eleven. She guessed the men still alive would soon be regretting that fact when the Dark Sons got them somewhere alone. The prisoners would be *persuaded* to spill all they knew about Petrov's plans as well as anything else they were asked.

She placed her sniper rifle back carefully into its specialized compartment in her trunk. Packing things up neatly took extra time but reduced the danger of not having quick access to what she needed in the future. Preparation was one of many keys to success.

Nadya tossed the RPG-7 haphazardly into the trunk and walked away. Diana shook her head. How could the two of them even be related? It took a little rearranging to make up for the space that would have been taken up by the HE warheads her niece had used so the weapon wouldn't slide around. Finally she was able to slide the false bottom of the trunk back into place.

"What the ever loving fuck?" Hawk's growled words were

followed by Nadya's squeal of excitement. Diana turned to watch her niece launch herself in a flying hug at her father's neck.

To give the man credit he didn't flinch at the surprise attack and caught his daughter before she could knock him over. Hawk's posture softened a bit as he squeezed her back. It was good to see them bonding even if it was over something so unconventional.

"I saved your ass, Daddio!" Nadya teased.

Two more men entered the small hidden parking area. Hannibal looked completely baffled by the nineteen-year-old's exuberance while Highdive's scowl was focused on her. It was as if he couldn't believe she was there and had been the one sniping from the ridge.

The look might have been insulting, but she guessed she could forgive him for needing time to come to terms with who she was. It was only fair. Diana had known everything there was to know about Highdive before she had approached him at the club. He'd only known the truth about her for less than twelve hours.

"Thought you were meeting with a contact." Highdive's voice was tight as if it was taking everything inside him to hold back some deep emotion.

Was he angry with her? Or was it something else? Was he accusing her of lying to him? That thought made her own anger rise, but she pushed it back and tried to think rationally. What would she think if their positions had been reversed? Diana closed the trunk and considered her words carefully.

"I did meet my contact. He told me that Tony was about to double-cross you all with an ambush."

"So instead of calling, you decided to drive up here and launch rockets at us?" Hawk growled.

She might be willing to cut Highdive some slack on his attitude, but Hawk should know better than to question her with that tone. Her sister would have shot him for snapping at her like an errant child. The man was lucky she had a less volatile temper than her sister.

Diana crossed her arms and glared at her brother-in-law, not intending to answer him until he found his calm.

"The rockets were me. And if I'd been shooting at you I wouldn't have missed. Aunt Diana was the sniper." Nadya raised her chin. "I think the words you're looking for, Pappy are *thank you.*"

Hawk pinched his nose and looked like his head might explode.

Diana decided to have pity on him before he had a stroke. "I met my contact here. We discussed him handing over information on Petrov. By the time he told me what was going to happen you were already pulling up."

"Very convenient meeting your informant right next to where we were getting ambushed."

The suspicion in Highdive's voice was technically reasonable, but it still stung. Did he really believe she could have been part of the ambush? Or that she would withhold critical information that could have killed him?

"No, I would have preferred to get the information a lot sooner. Then I would have eliminated the threat." She locked gazes with Highdive. "That's how I work. I don't make plans that rely on my niece to play Rambo with my most explosive toys."

"You could have been killed." The pain in Highdive's voice shocked her. Her anger melted like ice under the desert sun.

Could he be concerned for her safety? How... sweet. She'd never been the type of woman people tried to protect. She'd actually been the safest person in the battle since she'd been lying prone on the cliff edge but that didn't seem to matter to him.

How could she tell him she appreciated his concern

without undermining herself? She kept her voice soft. "You *would* have died. Honestly it's a miracle you survived even *with* our help. If Nadya hadn't used the rockets the way she did a lot of you still would have died."

Nadya blushed, but she stood a little straighter with the praise.

Highdive grabbed Diana's arm. "It's not your job to protect me."

Diana tried not to growl at the ridiculous statement. She shook off his grip and glared at him. "Is that your way of saying thank you?"

"Who was your contact?" Hawk cut into their argument.

The tension building between the two of them was like a rubberband ready to snap. It had been a long time since she'd allowed anyone to question her actions. Normally, if someone was stupid enough to try, she'd violently put them in their place then leave. Her sister probably wouldn't appreciate it if Diana badly damaged her husband.

A childish part of her wanted to let them know everything to justify her actions. Shifting the blame for the almost disaster onto the correct shoulders. But that wouldn't be professional. Whether she agreed with her client's decisions or not.

A client's confidentiality was sacred. Even when they acted like idiots.

Donavan Minetti had earned her respect a long time ago, but the games he played when his son was involved had gotten out of hand. Someone needed to talk sense into him. Since Diana preferred to remain alive, that someone wouldn't be her.

Nadya giggled. "It was some old guy. Never seen him before, but he was creepy."

Diana glared at her niece and tried not to laugh. Donavan Minnetti was many things but creepy wasn't one of them. Nadya also, without a doubt, knew who he was and apparently understood that his involvement wasn't knowledge that should be shared.

"What?" Her niece's shocked look was award worthy. "You didn't say I couldn't tell anyone."

It was good to know that the teenager could lie convincingly. Her niece had probably acquired that ability when she was very young to survive living with her grandfather. Nadya's youth and perceived innocence would be helpful in convincing these men she was the picture of virtue.

Diana almost pitied Hawk.

Grinder stepped out of the woods with a makeshift bandage wrapped around his arm. The injury didn't look too bad, but sometimes flesh wounds were more painful than more serious ones. The white blood-stained material was an uncomfortable reminder of how much worse events could have been.

"Tek says he can't reach you on comms. The police have received reports of possible explosions in this area. We have about forty-five minutes before someone shows up to investigate."

Body cleanup wasn't something Diana usually worried about unless a client required it. She used untraceable weapons and would be long gone before it mattered. However, this was the Dark Sons' territory. The mess down in the field could blowback hard on them. Over twenty-five bodies would be difficult to clean up even without the time constraint.

Hawk sighed. "Have Tek call in some of our markers and slow down or cancel the police response. Let's get the bodies into the truck and get it out of here as fast as possible. Contact Clean and ask where he wants them taken to. Is Minetti still down there?"

Grinder nodded.

"Okay, have him meet us back at the clubhouse and we'll

do a full debrief." Hawk looked at Highdive. "Do you want someone to ride your bike back to the compound?"

Highdive nodded.

Guess that meant she was going to have an extra passenger. Diana sighed. He would want to *talk*. Something she wasn't good at in the best of times.

Fine, she could admit they had a lot of things to work out. But starting those discussions now might derail everything else that needed to be done. She'd never had personal problems disrupt a job before and wasn't sure how to deal with it.

"I'm gonna ride with you, Pops. No way I'm getting stuck in that car full of awkward!" Nadya pouted with a bit more drama than was necessary.

Diana was glad for the distraction from her thoughts. "Don't think for one moment I've forgotten the stunt you pulled earlier. You and I will be discussing the consequences of not following orders, your pathetic concealment skills, and why you shouldn't fire off an RPG without warning the person next to you."

"Yes ma'am!" Nadya executed a sloppy salute. Yup. The girl was just like her mother.

Hawk shook his head. "Daddio? Pappy? Pops?"

Nadya smiled. "I figure I'll try out all the versions of male parental unit and see what feels right."

"Why not just use Dad?"

"Eh. Dad is boring. No one in this family is boring. "

Diana couldn't disagree with that statement. Though if she hadn't listened to her sister's stories over the years about Hawk she might have believed the man was as straight-laced as his combat boots. She looked over at Highdive, planning to share a smile at the ridiculousness of the situation, but saw he wasn't in the mood.

This wasn't going to be a fun car ride.

Chapter 13

We're not arguing. I'm simply explaining to you why I'm right.

The war between Highdive's head and heart was slowly driving him insane. He was not an indecisive man. Making hard choices was his damn job. So, why was he second guessing everything he did or said with Diana?

The danger she had put herself in was unacceptable. True, if she had followed his orders he and many of his Brothers would be dead. But what about next time? Her actions had blindsided him.

For months their relationship had existed in a bubble. Highdive loved the hours they'd spent together safe from the pressures of the outside world. It had felt natural, simple, and easy. She'd been a woman seeking the safety and comfort of submission. He'd enjoyed the challenge of getting her to let go. Of getting her to open up to him.

Now he realized how very little she'd told him. How many

false assumptions he'd made. Her unique mind drew him in. He'd smugly thought he'd figured her out.

He'd been wrong.

A normal woman would've started venting their frustration the minute the two of them were alone. Highdive had been prepared and even eager for that. An argument to let out the anger boiling inside him would have been a welcomed release. Unfortunately Diana was silent, her body relaxed and face serene.

How the hell did she do that? If she'd stayed silent and seethed it would have given him an opening to start the argument. But she looked as if she was out for a pleasant night drive. Her feelings so repressed, they might as well have not existed.

If they were at Dark Secrets he'd know what to do. Break her down with pleasure and pain until her control crumpled and she showed him what she was hiding. But at the Club she chose to let him have that level of control. Would she ever give him the gift of her submission outside those walls?

He didn't want or need her submission 24/7. Hell, one of the things he loved about Diana was the fire of self-determination that burned at her core. That until she'd disappeared he'd never been concerned that she needed more than he had to give. He enjoyed that each time she submitted it was a choice instead of a foregone conclusion.

Every moment she'd allowed herself to be vulnerable was special to him. But without that dynamic he didn't know how to make her open up and listen. She wasn't alone anymore. Her actions tonight could have had far reaching consequences.

Yes, without the two women, most, if not all, of the people down in the field would have died. But the reckless disregard for her own life terrified him. She acted as if any risk to her was acceptable. As if Diana believed her death would mean nothing, rather than being something that would destroy him.

She parked the car and Highdive realized his time to come up with the perfect words to get through to her had run out.

"Diana, you can't do things like you did tonight."

Not the most eloquent of arguments, but it stated his point.

Diana opened the door and slid out of her seat before turning to face him. "I obviously can, because I did."

Her eyes sparked with rage. He'd hoped to break through her calm, just not quite that way. Screw it. He'd take her anger if it meant she wasn't ignoring him. She slammed the door shut before he could respond.

Highdive got out of the car and jogged to put himself in her path. There was no way he was going to let her run away until she understood she couldn't take risks without considering the consequences. They were a couple and everything she did could affect the Club as a whole.

"That's not what I meant and you know it." The fight he saw in her eyes probably didn't bode well for him but he didn't care.

She cocked her hip. "Okay. What exactly did you mean?"

Putting into words every fear and horrible scenario he had imagined once he realized she'd been up on that ridge was difficult. That none of them had happened didn't matter. Just the possibility that she could have been hurt or worse tore him apart.

"You got lucky tonight, Diana. But if Petrov's men had figured out where you were, or if they had more men in the woods, you'd have been stuck up there with only a teenage girl as backup."

She lifted her hands up to her face like she was praying then dropped them with a huff.

"Luck? That's what you think kept me alive tonight? Why?

Because I'm a poor, defenseless woman who needs a big, strong man to keep me safe?"

He was making a mess of this. The last thing he wanted was to belittle her abilities, but being able to fight off a jumped-up Italian pretty boy or being a deadly shot with a sniper rifle didn't make up for years of training in tactics. It didn't give a person the skills necessary to survive a battle like tonight. That required a team and years of training.

Taking a deep breath he tried to backpedal a little. "I know you are very skilled with a sniper rifle. I saw that myself tonight. I also know it wasn't the first time you have killed someone. But being an assassin is not the same thing as being in a battle. You aren't trained for that kind of combat."

She snorted. "Do you know how old I was the first time I killed someone?"

Highdive shook his head, sure the answer to that question was going to piss him off.

"I was ten years old. I strangled the son of one of my father's soldiers with a sheet when he tried to crawl into bed with me." Her eyes seemed to glitter in the dim light. "I stopped counting the number of lives I'd ended when I was eighteen because it no longer mattered. Highdive, I'm twenty-eight and have been known and hired as Tishina for over fifteen years. What did or did not happen tonight had *nothing* to do with luck."

She had started killing for hire at age thirteen? Horrifying as that was, she still wasn't understanding.

"This isn't about your ability to kill. I'm saying you need to think before you act. Clear your plans with me ahead of time so you can have someone who has actual combat training as backup. Consider the consequences your actions might have on others." Highdive clenched his fists. "You threatened to start a gun battle in the middle of the Club-house because you wanted to meet some contact and wouldn't even discuss other options. That is completely unacceptable."

There was a chain of command in place for a reason. To ensure actions were thought out and coordinated. To keep people from recklessly putting their lives in danger.

"You know what's unacceptable?" Her voice practically hissed with emotion. "You thinking that you can keep me locked up in some sort of cage like a pretty bird. I'm not a pet!"

"I never said I thought you were a pet." What would it take to get her to understand he just wanted what was best for her?

"No? You say I have to clear my actions with you, consider the consequences. But does that order work both ways?" She raised an eyebrow. "I didn't think so, but you still think you can dictate my actions. How is that any different than a trained attack dog serving its master?"

Highdive shook his head. She was right to a point but... "You don't have the training that my Brothers and I have. You need to let me protect you, if you go tearing off when I can't back you up..." He threw his hands up into the air. "Do you realize it would kill me if something happened to you and I wasn't there to protect you?"

"*Kretin!*" Diana slipped around him so quickly he didn't have a chance to stop her. She stormed off towards the Clubhouse.

He wasn't sure what the Russian word she had shouted at him meant, but it probably wasn't flattering.

"Diana!" Highdive shouted, but the aggravating woman didn't even pause her stride.

The night air felt like ice against his skin. He tried taking a calming breath. Did his Brothers have these kinds of arguments with their women behind closed doors? He didn't think so.

Okay, none of the other Old Ladies had the skills that his did. They might have had hard lives but they didn't know what it was like to be the sharp end of the stick.

Only Max's woman, Cat ever showed even the slightest problem with the way things worked. She had been an undercover DEA agent before the Cartels ruined her career. She, too, had wanted to be kept fully in the loop.

Did he need to rethink how much he shared with Diana? This was what Hawk had been warning him about earlier. Could he treat her like he did his Brothers? Let her risk her life?

Rage at the thought burned in his gut. He took a deep breath and tried to calm down. It took a few minutes, but once he had himself under control he followed her inside.

Several of his Brothers and most of the Old Ladies were awake and scattered around the large main room of the Clubhouse. Of the men who had been at the battle tonight only Hawk and Sharp were present. They sat at a table with Nadya and Tomasso Minetti.

His Old Lady was standing at the bar next to Cami who had her laptop open. The two women seemed to be having an intense discussion. No one would know by looking at Diana that they had just been outside arguing.

When she finally looked up, she stepped away from the bar like a gunslinger getting ready for battle. Finishing their discussion in private was probably the wise thing to do. But that would give her the opportunity to walk away again. They needed to have this out now.

The way Nadya looked back and forth between the two of them was almost comical. The eye roll that followed was typical teen. "Damn it. You guys were supposed to work out your problems on the drive here. Why didn't you guys pull over somewhere and fuck it out or something?"

Most of the people in the room burst into laughter. Hawk's

daughter was a handful and Highdive was glad she wasn't his problem.

"Fuck it out?" Diana's voice held muted amusement. "Did your mother teach you that phrase?"

"Nope." Nadya popped the p. "Blame the internet and tech ignorant nannies. No one ever installed content filters on my computers."

Cami cackled and gave the girl an encouraging thumbs up. Hawk looked like he was struggling between annoyance and amusement.

"As amusing as your idea is, little rabbit. There are more important things to discuss." Diana gestured to the laptop. "I just gave Cami the location of the files my contact gave me. There was information on Petrov and several months of data from Tony's email and phone showing he had been working with the Russians for a while."

Tomasso slammed his fist on the table. "If you knew he had been working with the Russians for a while, why didn't you tell me?"

Highdive was glad the look Diana gave the Italian wasn't directed at him. It felt like the temperature in the room dropped several degrees. How was this intimidating woman the same person as the soft, sweet sub he had held in his lap so many times?

"For one, Mr. Minetti, I don't work for you. I do, however, occasionally work for your father. I've told him my concerns about Tony for years. Did he not pass them along to you?" The look she gave him said she knew he had.

"He did but—"

"But nothing," she cut him off. "You ignored your father because you thought he was being paranoid and Tony was your *friend*. You don't have the luxury to ignore warning signs like that Mr. Minetti. Until tonight I didn't have proof, or I would have shared it. I think what you meant to say was

'Thank you for stopping Tony from putting a bullet in my head.'"

Was his woman insane? It took brass balls and a death wish to be so hostile to one of the most powerful men in the Mafia.

The silence stretched as rage and frustration played across Tomasso's face before he nodded. "I apologize for my tone, Tishina. Thank you for what you did tonight. My family and I owe you a debt."

Tomasso's calm words and the sincere, if grudging, respect in his voice shocked Highdive. He would have bet good money that there was no way the Italian would be backing down publicly to anyone even if he was in the wrong. What kind of influence did Diana have that she could make someone like Tomasso apologize?

The silence stretched until she gave Tomasso the smallest of nods. Unease settled at the base of Highdive's spine. Why was she continuing to push the man? He really needed to talk to her before she dragged them all into a war with the Minettis.

Highdive decided to end the stare down. "Diana, we need to finish our conversation. Now."

Her gaze whipped over to him and he was glad looks couldn't kill. She looked like a warrior goddess descended to the Earth ready to slaughter her enemies. It was definitely not the time or place, but the lower half of him couldn't wait until the two of them could 'fuck it out' like Nadya had suggested.

"You want to finish our conversation, now?" She walked towards him like a leopard stalking its prey.

"Yes." The heat crackled between them and made him want to fuck her against the wall until she melted into him. If the situation wasn't so critical he might have acted on the impulse.

She put her hands on her hips, the motion drawing his

gaze down her wonderful body. "Fine. I'll summarize your argument for everyone to save us some time."

Privacy didn't appear to be an option. Fuck it. If their fight distracted attention away from her disrespect of Minetti he would willingly let everyone in on their disagreement. Knowing she would continue whether he wanted to or not, he nodded.

Diana's smile was anything but comforting. "You want me to clear with you anything I do that may be dangerous or have possible repercussions."

Why did she sound like he was being unreasonable?

"Yes."

"At the same time you intend to keep me in the dark, so I can't possibly know *if* what I'm doing might affect you. And if *you* determine something is dangerous, I will either not do it or I will allow you to assign someone to back me up. Someone who you say will have better training than me."

Nadya must have swallowed her drink wrong because she began coughing. The girl leaned forward, a shocked look on her face.

Highdive considered what Diana had said. She had summed up his thoughts rather neatly. The comment about being kept in the dark was a little dramatic, but he guessed he couldn't blame her for that. He could even understand her frustration. Maybe that was one point he could give to her.

Relationships were about compromise, right?

"I promise I won't keep you in the dark anymore. But yes to the rest of what you said."

Nadya groaned, then burst out laughing. What the hell did she find so funny? Everyone at her table was looking at him like he was insane. He didn't like it.

Hawk grimaced and shook his head. What was he missing? He looked over at Cami and even she seemed to be in on whatever it was the others knew.

The curvy hacker winced. "Did you t-take some time to read over the files I sent?"

"No." With everything else that had been going on that day he'd figured reading a background check on Diana was pretty low priority. Now he was wishing he'd had.

"So uhm... Diana's had like s-super spy training Russian style." Cami perked up. "D-do you know B-Black W-Widow? Like that without the mind control drugs... Wait, there weren't m-mind control drugs, were there?"

Diana snorted. "No."

"Darn. That would have been s-super awesome."

Highdive knew who they were talking about but not why. "Her training with a sniper rifle is impressive and I'm sure she's good with other weapons, but what does that have to do with my demanding she take military trained backup?"

Hawk answered, "What Cami is trying to say in her special way is Diana is more qualified than any of us to determine if or what she needs as backup. Hell, I've only met a few people who have even half the training she does. She's been learning this shit since she could walk. I'm pretty sure that instead of learning history and science in school she learned tactics and weapons."

Diana's laugh was bitter. "And instead of bad grades we got beatings and the only way to drop out involved a coffin. Highdive," her voice softened, "I don't specialize in easy kills that any trained sniper could perform. People seek me out for jobs that others consider impossible or too dangerous because I have the training and skills to survive and succeed."

The strength it must have taken to survive a childhood like that blew him away. How had he so underestimated her? Highdive wasn't sure he wanted to read her file. Not because he couldn't accept the fact that she might have more training than he, but because of the nightmares the information would cause.

It didn't change that he wanted to keep her safe. She might know when things were dangerous, but would she prioritize her life over making more money? He had no idea what her financial situation was, but in his mind, nothing was more important than she.

Tomasso chuckled. The mocking sound grated on his nerves. "You live more dangerously than I thought if you took her as a wife and didn't know all of this. Most of the families won't hire her because no one survives crossing her."

"Then why the hell did you try to have her punished for fighting with Tony?" Highdive asked confused.

Tomasso shrugged. "I would never have laid a hand on her and she knew it. There were a lot of witnesses, so I counted on her to play along. As soon as we were away from prying eyes I would have made Tony apologize and let her go her own way. Tishina knows how the game is played."

It felt as if someone had pulled back the curtain and he wasn't sure what was real anymore. How many things had he misread? Diana looked at him with pity as if she understood how much this was fucking with him.

"You knew?"

"I knew he was either going to do that or I was going to have to explain to his father why I had killed Tony and his son."

"Then why did you accept my claim?" It didn't make any sense. He had thought he had been saving her from them. Why would she have been willing to tie her life to his if she wasn't in danger? His heart felt like it skipped a beat and pain lanced through his chest.

Did she intend to leave him?

Chapter 14

Love is being obsessed with someone, but in a non-creepy way.

A nyone who says that love conquers all has been reading too many modern fairy tales. The reality is that relationships are complicated and take work. Love is a nebulous yet overwhelming emotion that is a prize for continuing to care even when things get hard. It is the reward for resolving your problems, finding compromises and finally connecting on a soul deep level with another human being.

Diana remembered the moment when Highdive laid his claim on her. She'd known that his declaration had been driven by fear for her safety. It had been unnecessary but sweet in a way she'd never experienced. For the first time in her life there was someone at her back who wasn't there because of family obligations or money but because they truly cared for her.

His chivalry alone wouldn't have been enough for her to

say yes. What had driven her to accept his claim had been the feelings developed through the months spent with him at Dark Secrets. Diana had thought she was going to lose him when her deception was revealed. So she'd grasped onto his claim like a drowning swimmer for just the possibility of something more.

Diana stepped closer to Highdive and placed her hands on his chest. She lifted her chin and looked into his eyes. He needed to understand what she was about to say. "I accepted your claim because I wanted to. Because you saw me as more than an assassin. You wanted me for who I am not what I am. Because with you I don't *have* to be Tishina. Sometimes I can be Diana or even Luna."

"Since I didn't even know you were an assassin, seeing you as something else wasn't that difficult." Diana could tell Highdive was trying for humor but the pain in his voice was hard to ignore.

She had been so focused on making sure Highdive respected her skills that she had forgotten to do the same. There had been good reasons she had reached out to him all those months ago. He was a protector who enjoyed ensuring those under his charge thrived. Would she really try to change that, no matter how annoying it could be?

To him her life and happiness was more important than what she could do for him. By not taking the time to explain, she had risked their relationship. Instead of talking, she had threatened him. How could he treat her as an equal in combat if she didn't show him that she deserved that respect?

She needed to remember that there was a part of him that wasn't a soldier, that wasn't the Sergeant of Arms of the Dark Sons. He was a man who cherished a woman. He was the man who would let the whole world drop away and focus completely on her if only she would hand over all her concerns to him.

Diana looked around the room and thought about the different relationships that existed within the unique club. Despite their lack of deadly skills the women in this room weren't weak. They showed their strength by being the anchors in the storms of life for their men. By creating a safe harbor where all of these soldiers could rest. Giving them purpose beyond survival.

Could she be like them? Did she want to be like them? Her time as Luna had changed her. Given her a reason to look to the future. She couldn't hand over everything she was and become someone new permanently. But that wasn't what he was asking for.

He was asking her to lean on him, like she wanted him to lean on her. Luna was as much a part of her as Tishina was. She wanted Master H as much as she needed Highdive. They were all part of the whole.

"I know I didn't tell you about that part of my life and I am sorry. It's going to take time and probably a few arguments before we find our version of normal. I wanted that then and I still want it. Even if I sometimes want to strangle you, I love you, Highdive."

He chuckled and cupped her cheek. His hand was warm and his eyes were soft with emotion.

"You terrify me. Not because I think you're going to strangle me, but because I don't know if you understand what anything happening to you would do to me. You're my Old Lady, the center of my world. When you disappeared it was like my reality was off center. The moment I saw you again I knew I couldn't let you go again. I love you, too."

Highdive kissed her and the world seemed to disappear. She clutched onto him and tried to show him with every part of her body that she wanted everything he was and would someday be. Love and passion, dominance and submission passed back and forth between them like swirls of wind in a tornado.

"Aww." Nadya's voice cut into their moment like a bucket of ice water. "That was hot and totally nothing I needed to witness. I don't mind you killing people in front of me, Aunt Diana, but I draw the line at watching you get freaky."

Diana bumped her head in frustration against Highdive's chest. Her family was so odd. He on the other hand was chuckling, the sound warm and comforting.

She was startled when he bent down and put his shoulder into her stomach lifting her off the ground. She barely stopped herself from fighting back and rolling away. Her head hung down his back and her sheaths of throwing knives dug into her stomach, but she had a spectacular view of his ass.

Highdive put a firm arm over her legs. "I think we're going to take this somewhere more private."

Diana ignored the laughs and whistles as Highdive carried her out of the room and up a flight of stairs. A strange sense of security filled her with every one of his confident strides as he carried her upstairs. Yes, she was armed and could take care of herself, but in that moment she didn't have to.

They entered a room with a black door and he slowly lowered her to the floor. Thoughts of the people downstairs faded from her mind as she took in the gorgeous man in front of her. His eyes practically glowed green in the dim light of the bedroom. He ran his hands up her arms to her shoulders and she shivered as his arms flexed.

"I will try to not treat you like you are helpless. It would be easy to say the only reason I did was because I didn't know. The truth is, knowing probably wouldn't have changed much, your safety means more to me than anything else." The sincerity in his voice melted straight through the remnants of anger that had held her muscles tight.

"I shouldn't have jumped right to threats. Being who and what I am means I'm used to reacting with brutality and extremes because that is all that most of the men I deal with understand. I don't want that with you. I need you to respect me but one of the things that I love about you is that I do trust you to be in charge." She looked up at him with a smile. "I hope you understand how rare that is. I don't even trust my sister in that way."

"Is that so?"

Highdive ran his thumb over her lips and her whole body trembled. How did this man make even the smallest of gestures feel so good?

"I told you from the beginning that I couldn't submit outside of the bedroom, but I will try to be more of a partner and talk things out with you. If you will promise to remember that I am a soldier not just a lover."

"I promise to try but you may need to remind me." His gaze grew heated as it ran down her body. He looked around the room and smiled. "Looks like we are in a bedroom right now."

"So we are." Diana bit back a laugh. It had been an intense night and the idea of letting go and letting him take control sounded perfect. She rolled her shoulders back and crossed her arms behind her back the way he preferred. "What would you have of me, Master H?"

He stepped back, the pleasure in his eyes gave her a sense of satisfaction that she never understood. "Strip for me, beautiful."

Diana followed his direction trying not to rush even though she wanted to. His gaze was like a phantom caress as she neatly placed her clothes and weapons on the dresser against the wall. Once she stood completely naked in front of him she let her mind relax into that place he had taught her to find. Where she narrowed her focus down to only him and the immediate surroundings.

Highdive circled her so closely the heat from his body warmed her. This was so much more intimate than being at the club. The small room didn't have much beyond the pine dresser and the utilitarian king size bed. There were no decorations except the gray comforter and single white pillow.

"Kneel."

Diana lowered herself to her knees sinking deeper into the scene. He was bigger than she when they stood but from this position she felt tiny. His large body was like a guard against the outside world. The sensation of his hand running through her hair was like a mixture of worship and comfort.

"May I taste you, Master?"

"So perfect like this." He stepped in front of her. She saw his erection straining against his jeans before he slowly undid the zipper and freed himself. He looked down at her like she was something amazing.

She opened her mouth knowing he wouldn't want her to do anything more. That was the amazing thing about their time together. Fucking downstairs had been unusual and exciting where she acted as the aggressor, but it was this freedom to just exist and feel that she needed like water on a hot day.

His cock slid slowly across her tongue and the salty taste was welcome. She relaxed and closed her eyes, loosening her throat, ready for anything he might do. He never rushed, often trying even her legendary patience. The silky texture of his dick, the slow motion as he worked in and out of her mouth was all she needed to focus on.

Highdive slid into her throat and paused. Diana swallowed around his tip taking in a large breath through her nose. He groaned and pushed in further and gripped the back of her head blocking off her ability to exhale. Primal panic flashed through her before she pushed it away. He would let her breathe or he wouldn't.

"So beautiful." His thumb brushed the tears that fell from her eyes as her body involuntarily reacted. "I remember how much you used to struggle with this. Your body was still, but there was calculation in your eyes. Now there is only acceptance. Like you would let me stay buried inside you until you passed out. Do you have any idea how much that turns me on?"

He made small thrusts before pulling out fully. The rub of him so deep within her where no one else had ever touched was exciting. Diana gasped in air and smiled.

"Get on your back on the bed, hands above your head, legs spread."

She rose and he gripped her by the back of the head taking her mouth in a kiss that seared her down to the bottoms of her feet. His chest rumbled in a growl as her hands clenched his shirt. Their kiss was exquisite chaos within the sea of control he always seemed to surround himself with.

Diana stumbled as he let her go and not caring about dignity scrambled onto the bed knowing whatever he had planned would be exactly what she craved. The comforter was cool against her heated skin as she got into position. Highdive was practically ripping his clothes off, his impatience turning her on even further.

He slowly approached the bed gloriously naked. She had never seen him like this and enjoyed the view of everything that was him. His tattoos were works of art scattered around his body. Each muscle stood out in relief and she had the urge to trace each one with her tongue.

His fingers lightly brushed down her arm as she lay in the position instructed. "You have no idea how much I want to tie you up and spend hours taking you to the edge until you are begging to come. To see all your careful control be replaced by wild need."

It wasn't hard to imagine what he wanted as he had done

it several times before. Chills ran across her skin as he traced the lines of the path the rope would follow. Across her chest and stomach down her arms and legs creating a lattice that would allow him to restrain her in any way he wanted. She both loved and hated edging as the orgasms were like nothing else but the torture of being close to coming was something almost indescribable.

Giving up control versus losing control. Only he could get her to agree to something like that. She wanted to feel him inside her now. Wanted to continue building the connection between them. There would be time for games later.

"I need you, Master."

He crawled onto the bed caging her body with his. He nipped at her ear and his words were a deep caress that seemed to vibrate into her body. "So impatient. Don't worry, beautiful. I won't tie you up tonight, but not because you asked. We could be interrupted at any moment so it's not safe. But the most important reason is that I want to taste every inch of you, then I need to claim you as mine. I won't wait for that."

Highdive bit deep into her neck and she screamed. The sharp sensation washed over her and she arched into him. He had taught her not to hold back in so many ways. In weeks he had undone what had taken years of training to learn. The sound allowed the pain to escape and left nothing behind for her but pleasure.

Diana lost herself as he bit down her body with possessive growls. Each bite teetered on the edge of overwhelming. She would be covered in marks by the time he was done and he seemed determined to leave no part of her untouched. She gripped the edge of the mattress doing her best to stay still, but it was impossible as he bit and soothed the most tender parts of her body.

Highdive pressed his cock against her core. "You are just

dripping for me, aren't you? There is no going back for us. You are mine."

"Yes!" Diana cried out as he thrust into her. The feeling of being filled washed over her in waves of pleasure.

Never before had he taken her like this. It was almost animalistic in its intensity. His hands gripped her wrists with bruising intensity as he thrust with deep powerful strokes. An orgasm built deep within her core as he growled his pleasure out above her. Every place he had marked her throbbed with her heartbeat and she lost herself to the moment.

There were no words, only sounds as they came together in a brutal rhythm. Nothing in her life had ever been this perfect. Their bodies might be moving, but it was their souls that connected on a level she hadn't known existed. She was his and he was hers. They would fight and struggle but none of that would matter. All that was important was nothing and no one would ever drive them apart.

She couldn't hold back anymore and white light exploded behind her eyes as she screamed out her orgasm.

Chapter 15

I lost my control. Offering a reward to anyone who finds it.

The knock at the door was an unwelcome way to wake up after a night spent losing himself in Diana. High-dive opened his eyes to two unwelcome sights. The first was the fact that the sun was barely above the horizon meaning that they'd gotten less than four hours of sleep. The second was his Old Lady pointing what he could only assume was a loaded VP9 at the door. Was she even awake?

"When did you bring a gun to bed?" Highdive asked, trying to force his body and mind into a fully awake state.

"When you took a nap after round two." She yawned, lowering the weapon but not putting it down.

Another knock sounded and he rolled out of bed. What-ever they were waking him up for had better be important. He yanked the door open with a growl.

"What?"

Grinder stood there, his grin too big to mean this was a

true emergency. It didn't matter how long they'd been friends. Highdive was going to kill his Brother if the man was just fucking with him.

"Sorry to wake you. Officers are meeting in Hawk's office in ten."

Highdive rubbed his forehead. How had he forgotten that they were in the middle of a war? He was usually the one hunting down people for meetings not the other way around. He couldn't regret a single moment of the time spent with Diana last night but he should have been strategizing with Hawk or getting sleep so he was ready. For the first time since he had taken the position he had a fleeting wish that he could hand off the responsibility to someone else.

"Yeah. I'll be there."

"Okay." Grinder's eyes widened. "Damn. Were you hurt in the fight last night?"

What the hell was he talking about? He was about to ask then saw that his Brother's gaze wasn't on him but behind him. Highdive looked back and saw that Diana was out of bed, by the dresser completely naked, and doing something on her phone.

"No," Diana answered distractedly.

Fuck she was beautiful. Sleek like a jaguar and completely unconcerned with her complete lack of clothing. Small and medium size bruises covered her body filling him with a possessive pride.

"She's fine." Highdive slammed the door in his Brother's face. "Diana. You're naked."

She looked up from her phone. "So are you."

He was, but that wasn't the point. "You knew someone was at the door."

"You're serious?" She looked at him with puzzled eyes then threw her head back and laughed. The sound was beautiful, rich and full.

"Yes." He wasn't mad so much as surprised.

"Honey. I've been naked at Dark Secrets in front of a lot more than one person. From what I've heard you all like to get freaky during parties. How is this," she gestured to her body, "bothering you?"

When put that way he couldn't help but join her amusement. "I guess it's not."

"Don't worry. I don't have plans to start running around naked, but I also don't care except for the fact it's harder to hide weapons without clothes."

He smiled considering the creative ways his woman would probably find to make sure she was armed even in the buff. Would there ever be a time when she felt safe enough to not consider weapons a mandatory part of her wardrobe?

The hours they had spent in each other's arms last night had not been enough. He wanted days alone with her where they had nothing to worry about except their mutual pleasure. Wrap her in silk rope and spend hours driving her out of her mind. Seeing her mindless with pleasure would be his reward.

"Don't you have to get to a meeting?"

Damn, he did. "You are too distracting."

There was no way he was going to get anything done if he continued to look at her gorgeous body covered in the marks of his passion. Maybe he owed some of his Brothers an apology. He'd ripped into many of them for losing focus over a woman and here he was just as bad. Highdive pulled on his clothes and was glad to see Diana was doing the same.

"That sounds like a 'you' problem."

"Is that so?" He pulled her in for a quick kiss. "You don't find me distracting at all?"

"I didn't say that. Go, I'm going to grab some food. When your meeting is over you need to bring me up to speed so I can let you know how I can help."

His knee jerk reaction was to tell her not to worry they had everything under control. It was going to take a while before his first instinct wasn't to shelter her. Thing was she might be able to help. She probably knew Petrov personally and would have better insight into what the man might do.

He nodded and headed out of the room as he heard her phone ringing. Who would be calling Diana this early? It was just one more thing he would have to learn about her. When he had time.

Highdive was glad to see he wasn't the last to arrive at Hawk's office. Grinder and Sharp were seated looking worried, but Dozer and Tek weren't there. Tek could be calling in but he doubted it. Since he'd stepped down from his position as CEO the Brother had been a lot more present and active within the Club. He gave a nod to everyone there and sat to the left of the President's desk.

It only took a few more minutes before everyone was there and seated. Surprisingly it was Tek who spoke first.

"We're getting chatter from across the country that something big has gone on with the Stepanov Bratva. The rumors are all over the place, but the one thing everyone agrees on is that the soldiers are all moving to consolidate their power with brutal tactics that have everyone, including their allies, turning on them."

A loud rap was followed by the door swinging inward. To his shock Diana, not one of his Brothers, stood in the doorway. Her face looked like it was carved from stone.

"Why bother knocking if you just burst in without waiting?" Hawk growled.

"My father is dead." Her voice was emotionless.

His first instinct was to give his condolences, but then he remembered who her father was and what that would mean.

He should have considered that as a possibility when Nadya was brought here that her mother might do something drastic. But they'd been focused on Petrov.

"I'm sorry to hear that, Darlin'. We are in the middle of somethin' right now, why don't you go talk to Val. Highdive will be out for you in a bit," Dozer said.

Highdive winced realizing that the last two days had been such a nightmare he'd not kept even the officers up to date on everything that had gone on. Hell, he didn't even know who knew what at this point.

Diana snorted.

Hawk sighed and leaned back in his chair. "Fuck. Okay really short version to catch everyone up. Nadya Stepanov is my daughter, her mother and my wife is Alena Stepanov. Diana is her half-sister. I'm guessing my wife decided to rid the world of her father and we are about to experience the fall out."

"I thought your woman's name was Akula?" Grinder spoke up.

"Think of it like a Russian road name. She is also Akula and I am Tishina," Diana answered. "She is also inbound. ETA less than thirty minutes. She said to tell you she was bringing Max and Cat with her."

Highdive was surprised. How had the two gotten here from Dallas so fast without contacting him? His questions would have to wait, they had more pressing matters. "How do you think Petrov will react to the news?"

"He won't wait to attack if he finds out and that won't take long. His only hope of retaining any power once the family's enemies start to act is to end this war with you quickly so he can focus on them."

"Any hope of him giving up or taking us out?" Tek asked.

"No," Hawk answered. "Not only is this personal, but if he backed down now he'd appear weak. He's been shouting to anyone who would listen for months that he would not only take us out but claim our territory and businesses. Last count he had brought in over thirty men with promises of power and wealth and those are only the ones we know about. They're greedy fucks who won't accept backing down for any reason."

Plans started flicking through his head as Highdive considered the different possibilities. They had forty-six Brothers here on the compound and at least twenty three non-combatants. Normally he would be confident to say that he could hold off any force with that number of Brothers and the weapons they had stockpiled but what kind of hardware Petrov had was still an unknown factor.

How far would the Russian be willing to go to act out his vendetta? Would he attempt a full on assault and risk drawing the attention of Civilians and law enforcement? The Dark Sons had bought the land out in the middle of nowhere because they wanted their privacy. The closest neighbor who wasn't a member of the club was over two miles away but an all out firefight might still draw attention even if it was just from passing motorists.

"He'll come at you as soon as he can with everything he has once he has confirmation. You need to get the children out of here," Diana said with a deadly type of calm.

"They'll be in the safe room in the basement," Tek said.

Diana crossed her arms. "This building will be the main target. Your walls are twelve inch reinforced concrete which is great against most weapons. An RPG-7 round like the ones Nadya fired last night will either punch a hole in the walls and destroy anything inside or disintegrate the stone. If I had to guess he will come prepared to bring this place down around you. If it was me and I didn't care about casualties... I would have a helicopter do a fast pass, use heavy artillery to take out most of the buildings and rooftop snipers, and then have my ground troops move in during the chaos. You will be so busy trying to dig out your vulnerable that your surviving numbers would be easy to take out. This isn't a street gang fighting you for territory. You've all been in the military think well-funded terrorist and you will be closer to the mark."

"If he did that the US government would be all over him," Dozer said.

"But you will be dead and are you sure of that? They have people in the government. Covering up something like this wouldn't be hard since you all so conveniently set up away from anyone who would demand answers once you were gone."

Diana's cold appraisal was a shock to all their systems. They had been operating in the civilian world for so long that they had forgotten the horrors that were possible outside of their protected bubble. The Dark Sons had property all over the country and forty-three chapters that would take them in without hesitation. But only if they could get them there safely.

Highdive shook his head. "I think we've waited too long. Anyone we tried to move would be vulnerable during transport. We know Petrov has a way to see who comes in and out of the Compound. Even if we sneak them out the back, the amount of Brothers we would have to send to keep them safe would leave us critically undermanned."

Sharp gave Diana a considering look. "You think he would attack our families if we sent them out in trucks?"

Diana nodded. "In a heartbeat. The old ways of family being off limits wouldn't even give him pause. Andre is a Bastard in both the literal and figurative meanings of the word."

Fuck. They needed a plan. Now.

Chapter 16

At this point I think some people were put on this earth to test my anger management skills.

"**M**oy Sestra, Moy Muzh, idi syuda!" Alena's overly enthusiastic demand for her sister and husband to get out here was loud enough to be heard even in the closed office.

Diana enjoyed the mixture of frustration and relief that showed on Hawk's face as he heard his wife's shouted demand. Alena could speak flawless English when she wanted, which wasn't often. It was as if she enjoyed playing up to the Russian stereotypes. Loud, brash, and completely over the top was her default setting whenever there was a group of people around.

It was as good of a time as any to pause in the strategy session. Diana had never been in the position where she needed to defend someone other than herself. She understood the tactics used by those in security because she made her living going through them to her target. Working with the Dark Sons was a fascinating exercise where she told them how she thought Petrov would attack and the men adjusted their plans accordingly.

Already the children and their mothers had been moved into Tek's house further back on the property. His home was the most defensible and could hold all the people necessary. She would have preferred to evacuate them completely, but Highdive had pointed out the dangers involved. All that was left was small details that would probably have to change once things got hot.

"My sister has summoned us," Diana told Highdive then headed toward the main area of the Clubhouse.

Much to her annoyance, her niece was in the middle of a heated discussion with Alena when she entered the room. Standing by the door were two other people. She recognized Max and Cat from their pictures in her files. As per the new plan no one else was in the room. Most of the Brothers were scattered around the property in strategic locations. They were now using the garage as a centralized point rather than the Clubhouse.

Diana gave Nadya a disapproving glare. "You are not where you were assigned."

"I am not a baby who needs to be protected," Nadya growled. "I helped you last night. I won't let you bench me."

Alena laughed, obviously proud of her daughter's fighting spirit. Diana may have been the younger sister but she often felt like the mother when the two of them were together. Maybe it was time for her to not be the responsible one.

"You know what? It's not my problem. If you want to throw yourself into harm's way and possibly be the reason people die then take it up with your Mother and Father. From now on, I am going to be the fun aunt who takes you on shopping sprees."

Both Alena and Nadya looked at her like she had lost her mind. Maybe she had but her time with Highdive had made her realize that she didn't want to always be the responsible one. That everything in life wasn't life or death. Well, in this situation it was but the point was still valid.

"You hate shopping," Nadya said.

"I never said what I was going to take you shopping for," Diana teased back. It wasn't the shopping that bothered her so much as the complete vulnerability that walking through a mall represented.

"What the Fuck are you all talking about?" Hawk strode into the room apparently not in the mood for small talk.

"*Sladkiy sakharok!*" Alena ran across the room and threw herself at her husband like a squirrel jumping onto a new tree.

Diana couldn't help but chuckle. Hawk was so far from 'sweet sugar' that it was ridiculous. Max and Cat were laughing as well.

Highdive stepped up behind her and leaned in. "Hawk said you two looked alike but I never imagined just how much."

Alena peppered Hawk's face with playful kisses and Diana wasn't sure if the stern man was going to throw her sister off or continue to sit there like a statue. To her surprise, the man softened and then gripped his wife by the back of the head and kissed her with enough passion to heat up the room a few degrees.

In a strange sort of way the two of them worked. As if they existed on opposite ends of the spectrum balancing each other out in a way that nothing else could. Diana had only seen them together a few times, but she had always known that underneath the fiery clashing of wills the two both loved and respected each other.

"Okay enough!" Nadya made a gagging noise. "I'm already going to need enough therapy to send some head doctor's kids through college. No need to add the trauma of watching my parents get down and dirty."

"You are nineteen not nine," Alena scoffed. "Get used to it or learn to close your eyes. When we are done killing lots of people I plan on making up for years of lost time."

Hawk chuckled and touched his forehead to his wife's before putting her back down on her feet. He shook his head, then seemed to pull in on himself, going back to the serious man Diana was used to seeing. He gave a head nod to the two newcomers.

"Good to see you, Max, Cat. What do you all know?"

Max smiled. "We've been tapped into most of Petrov's electronic communications for the past day or so. Your Old Lady has a man on the inside as well. They are already gearing up to head this way. I think you have two hours at the outside."

"He won't wait until nightfall?" Highdive asked.

Cat shook her head. "They know you have access to helicopters and are on the verge of firming up alliances. They want to catch you off guard. And they have men hidden outside the compound to take out any air support."

"The *mudila* thinks he can actually replace my father." Alena shook her head.

Diana sighed. "Did you leave anyone else alive who could realistically take over?"

"Well, no. But that is beside the point. The man was barely on the edges of the inner circle. And he brought in outsiders to fight for him rather than our soldiers."

Hawk rubbed at his eyes as if fighting off a headache. "Our soldiers? Please tell me you aren't planning on taking over for your father."

"Nyet." The word was filled with vehemence. "I am retiring. I will make a good house wife for you."

Diana snorted, she couldn't help it. The indignation on

her sister's face unlocked something inside her. Diana threw back her head and laughed. The sound was contagious and soon most of the people in the room joined her.

"Mom, do you even know how to use a stove?" Nadya giggled.

"Bah! I will learn." Alena winked.

"Okay enough." Hawk probably had meant to sound stern, but he just sounded exasperated. "We are going to head over to the garage and get everyone up to speed. You," he pointed at Nadya, "will go back to Tek's place."

"*Papochka!*" Nadya's voice held more whine then she probably intended.

Hawk's eyes softened, but his face remained stern. "You can have a rifle. Your job is to help defend the kids. If you stray off your assignment again, I will lock you in one of our cells until this is done. *Ponimat*?"

"Yes, I understand." Nadya strode away in the teenage equivalent of stomping her feet.

"Is that what we have to look forward to someday? Are you going to make me be the bad guy with our kids?" Highdive whispered into her ear.

The idea shocked Diana. She had never considered having a baby. Not just because she hadn't ever had a serious relationship, but because she didn't think she was the type of woman who would make a good mother. Was that still the truth?

Could she picture herself raising a child with Highdive? He would make a good father even if she imagined he'd be painfully overprotective. She still wasn't sure she'd be a good mother but the idea wasn't as impossible as she once believed. It wasn't the time for life altering decisions like that, but she could tease him.

"Kids? How many do you think you can handle as a stay at home dad?"

Highdive looked as if she had hit him in the face with a

fish. She gave him a kiss on the cheek, then walked away to let him stew on the idea for a bit. She joined her sister who was heading out the door with the woman named Cat.

The ex-DEA agent gave her an up and down look. "Rambolina didn't say she had a clone. I'm Cat." The woman held out a hand.

Diana took it with a smile. "Rambolina. I like that. But we are just half-sisters, not clones. I'm Tishina, nice to—"

"Your name is Diana. Cat is a friend, not a client," Alena interrupted.

"It is a habit. You and Nadya were the only ones who ever called me Diana."

"But things change and we are both married women now."

"You and Highdive are married? Damn, you work quick."

"Please ignore my sister. I'm his Old Lady. Unlike her I didn't get my man drunk, drag him to a chapel, convince him to pretend to get married for fun, then file the paperwork and not tell him for two years."

Alena laughed. "Such sweet memories."

"You did that?" Cat asked.

Diana smiled. "When we're not under immediate threat I'll give you all the dirt on her."

"This is not fair. You are boring. I have no good stories to share about you that don't end in blood and violence."

"Tishina, that means silence right?" Cat asked.

"See, even her moniker is boring." Alena moaned.

"Because 'Shark' is so much more exciting."

"You guys are a trip. Where are the rest of the Old Ladies?"

Diana looked around before answering. The men were about fifty feet behind them having their own discussion. They were almost at the garage but she didn't want to risk giving anything away if Petrov had a way to listen in. "They've been put in a secure location with the kids."

"None of them wanted to help?" Cat seemed shocked.

Diana laughed remembering the snippets of fights she had overheard while they were scrambling to get everyone moved. "Wanted to, yes. But it was determined they didn't have the skills necessary to help in a more active roll."

"Is that a polite way to say their men said no?" Cat sounded upset.

It wasn't hard to understand why she would be offended, but Diana had agreed with the decisions. While most of the women knew enough about how to shoot to be useful in a pinch, the kind of fighting they would soon see would test even a soldier's ability to stay calm. She had even agreed to take a back-up role since she didn't have experience working with a unit. Her place would be as a roving asset patrolling the area near the houses.

Alena chuckled. "Probably."

"They had better not try that shit with me, or Max is going to find out what weeks of celibacy feels like," Cat grumbled.

With so little time to plan it was going to be interesting to see how the Dark Sons utilized the new arrivals. Diana caught her sister's gaze. They both knew that any threats that involved future punishment were a waste of air. People were going to die. Probably a lot of them. It was their job to make sure the majority of those people were on the other side.

Chapter 17

Okay, I'm here... what are your other two wishes?

"**D**amn it is good to have you back." Highdive gave Max a slap on the back as they walked into the garage.

He hadn't liked the decision to fake his Brother's death but understood the necessity. It had given the club time to prepare. They had spent the months since securing their businesses from outside interference. Making sure families knew what to do in an emergency, and making sure no one they cared for was ever alone and vulnerable to attack.

Never once did he give more than a passing consideration to a full-on assault. They had planned for drive-bys, people trying to sneak in, or trying to infiltrate the parties. There were over ten different contingencies for kidnapping or blackmail. Highdive thought Hawk might have suspected the Russian was crazy enough for a full scale attack but there wasn't much that they could really do to prepare for something like what was happening.

"Good to be back." Max smiled.

"Grinder will probably throw a party once this is over. He never wanted to be an officer."

"I have to admit I didn't see that one coming. He's a good choice though." Max took a deep breath. "But Cat and I aren't staying."

"No shit? What are you enjoying the Texas heat?"

"No, but she has too many memories here. I'll probably go nomad for a while until we decide where to settle. Cat talked about taking up private security work or private investigation. She isn't the type of person who enjoys the quiet life."

Highdive stole a glance over at Diana. That was something they were going to have to discuss. Listening to her earlier as she tore apart plan after plan had opened his eyes to just how much he still had to learn about her. They were an equal match on tactics, her mind working lightning fast to come up with new and inventive ways to approach the problem.

Her comment earlier about him being the stay at home dad had deflated his ego and shown just how many assumptions he had been making. His comment about kids had been meant to be a joke. He had never even considered kids. One thing was clear, they would need to have a lot more conversations before even considering it.

"Yeah. Don't know if you've heard but my woman isn't exactly a wallflower."

"Pussy is not supposed to be complicated!" Max had dropped his voice in a bad imitation of Highdive.

"Fuck you. Yeah, Karma has definitely kicked me in the balls for all the shit I gave you Brothers."

"Max!" Tek got out of his seat and strode over to them

giving the Brother a back slapping hug. "It is so good to see you."

"Well, I am pretty awesome." Max raised his arms and turned in a circle. "I mean with all this awesome here, you all can just sit back and relax."

Highdive had missed his Brother's relaxed and casual humor. He had always had the ability to make you feel like things were going to turn out fine. The only time he ever lost that laid back charm was when someone was insulting or endangering a woman he cared for. Highdive had been on the receiving end of his right hook once when he had insulted Sharp's Old Lady Pixie.

The backroom of the garage had been transformed into security central. There were almost twenty monitors stacked on different shelves cycling through live images of different parts of the compound. There were four drones ready to fly once things got started. Cami would control those from her safe location and act as backup in case Petrov's men took out this building.

"Max!" Cami's voice came through the speakers. "Is C-Cat with you? Val is going to l-lose her shit!"

Max looked around then laughed when he saw Cami waving to him from one of the lower monitors. "You are looking good as always. I'll send her—"

Alarms blared from the computer and Tek slid into his seat. How the man could type so fast was a mystery. Everyone held their breath as screens cycled quickly through different feeds.

"We've got a breach in the fence on the west side of the compound. Smoke, Rooster you are the closest I'm sending the coordinates," Tek fired off. It took a few seconds but finally the large screen on the wall gave a view of the area in question.

On the edge of the wide shot it was obvious that a section

of the fence had been cut away. Unfortunately, it was only partially visible but Highdive could see several men making their way through the break. He counted at least four but it was obvious that off to the left there were probably more.

Highdive ran for the staging area to grab a rifle and ammunition. The outer compound was his responsibility and the two Brothers could not handle that many men alone. How many should he take with him?

Diana was waiting for him in the room fully armed and ready. This had been their compromise. He wouldn't try to bench her, but she would work with him and follow his orders.

"Six men have broken through to the west. Smoke and Rooster plan to shadow until backup arrives," Diana said as he slung his rifle and clipped on an ammunition belt.

"How do you know?"

She tapped her ear then handed him an earpiece.

He slipped the device in. "Thanks."

"They won't be the only ones coming in through the back. Hopefully they will be heading towards the Clubhouse and not making any stops."

The houses weren't between the breach and the Clubhouse so he wasn't concerned about them endangering anyone yet. Luckily Tek had long ago wired most of the grounds with cameras and trip wires. They had seemed pointless when all that had ever been caught was wildlife but his forethought was really paying off now.

'Outer scouts have five armored SUVs heading our way less than ten minutes out,' Hawk's voice rumbled over the com.

'Drones are launching to do a sweep of the p-perimeter to see who else we have trying to sneak in the back d-door,' Cami's voice was calm and cool.

Highdive keyed his mic, 'I'm heading west, Smoke and

Rooster continue shadowing and wait for Diana and me if you can before you engage. Everyone else hold position.'

He had four Brothers and a prospect covering the Northern perimeter. Gears and Decaf were to the east. Hannibal, Ink, and Dragon were covering the house the Old Ladies and Children were in from sniper perches. Nadya had hopefully made it back to the house and would take up a defensive position.

'Stay tight and keep your heads on a swivel,' Hawk commanded.

Highdive jumped on his bike expecting Diana to climb on behind him. Instead she jumped on a cherry-red softail he had never seen before.

"Where the fuck did you get that?" Highdive asked as he kicked his bike to life.

She smiled as she started up the Harley. "My sister is staying here with Hawk she won't mind me borrowing it."

They raced off across the field. Riding the motorcycles killed any hope of stealth but the compound was just too large to remain on foot and have any hope of covering the distance effectively. He had thought riding into combat with Diana would have felt wrong.

It went against every instinct he had to be bringing her into danger with him. But seeing her riding focused beside him erased most of those feelings. Like she was one of his Brothers he had confidence that they would have each other's backs.

'We've got six men trying to cut through the northern fence with what looks to be a combat knife and two separate groups of four doing the same to the east. At the rate these idiots are moving it might take them a while but they all have ATVs so once they get through we have less than five minutes before they can reach the houses. It looks like they are packing more than just rifles on those things.' Tek paused in his update. 'I've got a positive ID on at least two of the men. They're wearing fucking Bloody Blades colors.'

Damn it. He had known those assholes couldn't be trusted. Highdive braked and Diana stopped beside him. His Brothers to the north and east would need their backup more than Smoke and Rooster. The ATVs and whatever they were carrying changed the equation. There were more enemies to the east but north they could use the road to close in fast.

The plan had been simple. Use a quarter of the Dark Sons forces to patrol the outer territory and pick off anyone trying to sneak in. They had hoped that since Petrov only had forty men he would focus on the Clubhouse. They would use that focus to pull him in and take him out from the sides.

But with the BBs in the mix that was a possible addition of twenty men. Not quality men but they were well armed and probably tweaking on their own product.

'Smoke you two are on your own. Get behind them and take them out if you can or meet up at the rally point with force at the range.'

'Rodger.'

"You go East, I'll go North," Diana shouted over the noise of their bikes.

"That wasn't the deal." Fear and anger raced through him like Olympic level athletes. She had agreed to stay with him and follow his orders and here she was at the first opportunity trying to rush off.

"But you know it is the right decision. I'll follow your orders like I promised but really think before you choose."

Damn it, she was right, but he couldn't say the words. If he sent her off on her own and she got killed he would never be able to forgive himself. Highdive wanted to scream his frustration to the skies and tell fate to go fuck itself. He needed to make the right call.

If he kept her with him simply because he didn't trust her

skills would she ever forgive him? If people died that she could have saved it would be almost as bad as if he lost her.

'They've breached to the north and the men to the east are almost through. Crash and Rubble are moving to engage.' Tek's voice cut through his inner monologue.

"Don't die." They were the hardest two words he had ever forced out of his mouth.

Diana gave him a short nod. "I love you, too." She raced off towards the woods and his heart felt like it was going to beat right out of his chest.

He turned his own bike around and headed to the east. Praying every second that he hadn't made the wrong choice.

Chapter 18

The Devil whispered, "I'm coming for you." I whispered back,
"You better bring tequila."

There was the unmistakable sound of gunfire coming
from deeper in the woods. Diana had spent long hours
studying the layout of the compound months ago but
there wasn't much information on the dirt roads that ran through
the forest at the back of the property so she hoped the path she
was on would take her to where she was needed. She would ask
for assistance but the updates and chatter on the earpiece had
reached an almost constant stream that she had to block out.

Petrov had breached the front gates and was being pulled
into the trap that awaited him there. Men were injured but she
didn't know who was where so the names weren't of much
help. The truth was she didn't have much of a plan except get
within visual distance of the firefight.

She had a Tavor X95 assault rifle slung across her back

but it wouldn't do her much good while riding. She was decent on the motorcycle but she couldn't ride without at least one hand on the handlebars. Even with her rifle's blocky bullpup frame without both hands she wouldn't hit shit. The chatter in her earpiece cut out.

Had she lost reception?

'There is a trail coming up on your left, 'darlin, if you take it you'll circle behind those gelded sons of milk cows.' The southern twang surprised her and she slowed.

'Val?' Diana saw the turn off on the left and took it.

'Got it in one. Cami has us on a private channel so I can talk you in. Crash is down and we think dead. From what we can see on the drone, Rubble, Blue, and Crow have them temporarily pinned but may have been injured as well. I'm gonna need you to live up to all that hype and get our boys out of there safe.'

'What is the situation?'

'Six assholes with guns shooting at our three who are using the trees as cover.'

Diana dodged a tree branch trying to maintain her speed without losing control. She took a deep breath.

'That isn't helpful. Fully automatic or semi? Are they in cover or out in the open? Will I be coming in behind them, in front of them, or to the side? Any chance I could sneak up on them?"

The sound of the gunfire grew significantly louder. She was probably going to come up on them in under a minute. She stopped the bike.

'What are you doing? You will come in behind them, just drive up and kill them all.'

Val's voice was full of anger and Diana shook her head slinging her rifle around to the front. The woman had obviously seen too many action flicks if she thought that kind of accuracy was even possible on a motorcycle in anything outside a movie or a practiced and planned stunt.

Keeping her movements slow and smooth she moved forward towards the sound of gunfire. She tuned out the creative and very southern insults that Val was sending her way through the earpiece. In any fight her perception of the world narrowed and broadened in complicated ways.

Short controlled fire that she assumed was the Dark Sons was echoed by wild bursts of fire. Given enough time the enemy would probably run out of ammo since they didn't seem to be taking any time to aim. But all it would take was a lucky shot to end a life.

After sliding around a tree, Diana paused as the combatants came into view. The scene crystalized like a snapshot in her mind. Six men in a staggered line on the road hunkered down behind their ATVs. They howled like animals as they fired wildly at the tree line in front of them. Three large trees were almost stripped of their bark from the amount of bullets that had been shot into them. She couldn't see them but guessed that was where the Dark Sons were taking cover.

On the motorcycle she would have only had seconds to try and aim and fire at these men. Her breath evened out as she sighted and aimed at each man. Running through the sequence of fire she intended twice. Air eased out of her lungs and time raced forward as she pulled the trigger rapid fire attempting to double tap each one.

Four of the six men's heads exploded with the impact of her rounds. Two had moved and only received body shots. She dropped the rifle on it's sling and pulled her VP9 on muscle memory. Diana glided forward, she was more accurate with a pistol at this range while moving. The first man clutched at his chest completely unaware of her approach and she ended him with one shot to the chest and two to his head.

The second saw her and tried to point his rifle towards her

but she shot him in the leg and he crumpled. Twice more she fired and he stopped moving when his brain could no longer send signals to his body. She approached the line of prone men who were wearing Bloody Bones cuts with caution. One by one she made sure they were dead feeling for a pulse even on the ones with parts of their skulls missing.

'Diana,' Val's voice was hesitant, 'I would like to apologize for any name I may have called you in the heat of the moment. I'm cooler than February morning in the mountains when it comes to medical emergencies but I may not be best suited to gunfights.'

Diana laughed and keyed her mic. 'That's okay, Val. I wasn't listening to you anyway. Can you give me an update on Highdive?'

'Sure thing, darlin', give me a minute.'

A man walked towards her from the tree line. He had dark hair and sharp features that did nothing to hide his scowl. The man she thought was named Blue was trying to hide a limp but wasn't being very successful. He looked over the six dead men his eyes widening.

"You're Highdive's Old Lady?"

She nodded, not sure why that was important.

"That was impressive. You saved our asses." The short compliment was probably the most she would get in the way of thanks. Not that she expected anything more. In her experience military service inhibited a man's ability to voice much more than curses or commands.

"Anyone else alive?"

"Gears is dead. Rubble is bad but should survive, Crow is stabilizing him."

She had never met Gears and didn't know much about him except he had an Old Lady who was probably back at Tek's, completely unaware that her husband was dead. Fortunately that wasn't her problem.

"Do you know what's going on?" She nodded to his earpiece. "Val hijacked my comm so I haven't heard any updates for the last ten minutes."

"They've got Petrov pinned down in an active crossfire in front of the Clubhouse. He's got grenades, several RPGs and automatic weapons so no one can get close. The coward is hiding behind his armored car refusing to retreat but also won't stick his head up far enough that someone can hit it. The west incursion was cleared and Hannibal and Sharp are managing to hold off the fuckers to the east."

A tight band that had been squeezing her chest loosened.

"What about Highdive?"

'Diana?' Val's voice held a tightness that she didn't like. She held up a finger to Blue and pointed to her ear.

'Yes, Val?'

'Don't worry we're working on it, but it seems no one can get Highdive on his Comm. And no one has reported seeing him since you two separated. We do have a ping on his phone, but we can't spare anyone to go check it out right now.'

She sprinted back towards her bike not bothering to acknowledge Blue. 'Give me his location.'

'It's probably just a technology glitch. You know those happen all the time. I'm sure he's fine and all this worry will be like dandelion fluff on the wind and we'll laugh like a hyena on a bender.'

Diana put all of her fear and rage into her voice as she jumped on her motorcycle. 'Val, where is he?'

Chapter 19

Some days, the supply of available curse words are not
enough to meet my demands.

His vision swirled between painful bright white and
darkness as if the world was being lit by a powerful
strobe light instead of the sun. Gravity seemed to
be acting oddly since parts of his body felt so heavy they were
unmovable. What the hell happened?

He'd been riding towards the eastern perimeter and had
broken through the tree line when an explosion knocked him
from his bike and sent him flying. He was under attack! Highdive struggled to get his brain online because his life might
depend on it. Everything hurt but he didn't think anything was
broken.

After a few moments he could feel the damp grass, cool
against his face. The muffled sounds of gunfire told him the
action was too far away to have been what took him out. So

what had? Fuck, it was hard to think with his ears ringing and the world spinning like he'd just stepped off the tilt-a-whirl.

Highdive felt more than heard someone quickly closing in on him. He forced his eyes open and rolled hoping to catch whoever it was off guard. Dirt kicked up into his face as a bullet buried itself in the dirt next to his head.

That was too close.

He lurched to his feet and charged the man who had fired. It was the fucking President of the BBs.

"Motherfucker," Breaker growled as Highdive tried to wrestle his rifle away.

The weapon pressed between them, the idiot started firing. The only thing that accomplished was Highdive's ears started ringing and the Ruger AR-556 ejected hot casings into Breaker's face. When the man squealed and tried to jerk back, Highdive laughed and held on. Despite that he kept firing until the weapon clicked empty.

Highdive drove his elbow across the man's temple and reached for his Glock. Fuck. The fall must've knocked the weapon free because his holster was empty. Now he understood why Diana had so many backups.

Hopefully she was doing better than he was. Not that he had time to worry about her with this asshole determined to take him out. Guess he was just going to have to kill the man the old fashioned way.

"Motherfucker!" Breaker spat blood and took a step back. The BB raised his assault rifle as if it still had ammunition.

"You already said that," Highdive taunted as he readied himself to attack. "I knew you were stupid, but only knowing one curse word is pathetic even for you."

"Fuck you and your Club! We're going to burn this place to the ground and make your women our bitches."

Holy shit was this man delusional.

"My woman would have you pissing blood before you ever

laid a hand on her." That was if she let him live that long. "I don't think this is going to turn out the way you think. You're out here alone without your boys. Pointing an empty rifle at me. Most of the sick fucks you call Brothers are already on the express train to Hell and you are about to join them."

Highdive rushed at Breaker pivoting and kicking at the last minute when he saw the man had dropped the rifle and pulled a knife. The BB stumbled back almost tripping when the barrel of his rifle got caught between his legs. With a scream of frustration the BB lifted the sling over his head and tossed away the weapon. His eyes were wide and jittery like a rabid animal backed into a corner.

Highdive forced himself not to rush. Untrained fighters were too often more dangerous than skilled ones. They would do things that made no sense and get in a lucky shot. On the mat that could be painful. Out here it could be deadly.

It didn't help that his balance was still off from the explosion and crash. If he was going to make sure he was the only one who walked away he needed to be smart. Breaker took wild swings with his knife as they circled each other keeping Highdive from getting too close.

The matte black of his Glock caught his eye. It was only a few yards away. Highdive dove for the gun as Breaker charged him. The pain of metal biting into his leg was only a minor distraction. The knife wound wasn't deep enough to stop him from rolling to his feet.

The BB's president snarled but froze as he looked down the barrel of the weapon.

"Throw away the knife and get on your knees," Highdive shouted.

Breaker dropped to his knees with a glare.

What the hell was he going to do with a prisoner? For the first time since he'd regained consciousness Highdive took the time to look around. About twenty yards away his bike was a mangled wreck. Next to it was an ATV he didn't recognize. His comm was missing so he couldn't call for backup. Maybe the ATV had something in the saddlebags that he could use to tie this asshole up.

The gunfire that had been close by had stopped. Hopefully that meant Sharp and Hannibal had taken out the rest of the crew who had broken through the eastern fence. The sounds of distant battle had slowed too. It was obvious there was still fighting going on near the Clubhouse but hopefully that would be over soon as well.

From the left came the roar of a motorcycle approaching at speed. Please let it be one of his Brothers. The bright morning sun glinted off the crimson paint almost making it look like the bike was about to catch on fire. Diana's usually neat braid was a mess of loose, brown curls that whipped behind her as she rode like she was at the head of a demon army.

Something in his chest relaxed. She was alive. Everything would be okay. Somehow he knew together there wasn't anything they couldn't handle.

That was if she didn't run him over.

The crazy woman skidded to a stop less than five feet from him and launched herself into his arms. It was as if she didn't even notice the gun he had pointed at the man kneeling less than ten feet away. He caught her with his free arm and tried not to stumble or groan in pain. His ribs were bruised along with the rest of him from the crash.

The minute her lips touched his none of that mattered. She owned him body and soul and nothing as insignificant as bruises or a tiny knife wound was going to dim the passion between them. She clutched onto the back of his head with one hand as their tongues dueled in the most primal of ways.

A gunshot shocked him out of the spell she had cast and he looked over expecting Breaker to have found a weapon while he had been distracted. The man's sightless eyes met his and Highdive scowled at Diana.

"You shot him?"

She shrugged, her legs still wrapped around his waist and her weapon already re-holstered. "He was crawling for his rifle."

"It's out of ammunition."

"How was I supposed to know that?" Diana nipped his neck. "Do you really care?"

Did he? There was very little chance that they would have let him live after what had happened here today. It was doubtful the man had any useful information so really she had saved him a lot of hassle. "I guess I don't."

She licked at the shell of his ear sending a shiver down his spine and making his cock go painfully hard. "You let me fight without you. I wasn't sure you would."

"I wasn't sure I would either." He ran a hand over her wild hair. "I still don't like the idea of you in danger, but I do trust you to take care of yourself. I love you, Diana." He took her mouth with a kiss that tried to say everything he felt. The world slipped away for a moment and it was just the two of them sharing a passionate moment.

He pulled back with a sigh. "Probably not the right time for this."

She smiled. "Why not?"

He raised an eyebrow and lifted her off him and back onto her feet. "I can still hear gunshots towards the Clubhouse. We're wearing armor and I don't know if there are more enemies on the grounds, or if everyone at the house is okay."

She stepped back and gave him a smile that could tempt a priest to sin. "Armor comes off. I still have my comm so I'll know if they need us. Hawk and my sister have things covered at the Clubhouse and no one got within fifty yards of the house with the women and children."

All of his training flew out the window. As she backed away from him. There were so many reasons that they shouldn't get distracted. So many things he had to get done. He should check on his Brothers. Get a casualty count. Make sure that all the families were safe.

But as Diana gave him her sensual smile and dropped to her knees, none of those things mattered. With her back to him, the tempting siren hooked her fingers under the belt at her waist and slowly dragged her pants down over her hips. The sight of the pale gorgeous flesh of her ass as she looked over her shoulder at him caused him to groan in defeat. Fuck it, his Brothers could wait.

The hunger in her eyes matched his own as she dropped to all fours revealing the pink folds of her pussy. Moisture glistened between her legs and he no longer cared about anything except getting her wrapped around his cock. Highdive strode forward undoing his own belt.

For too many years he had believed that finding his perfect partner meant being with someone who slid into his life seamlessly. It was a comfortable delusion where nothing in his life changed. She wouldn't have differing opinions or cause him to question his own actions. In other words, boring.

Diana had taught him that a good partner pushed you to be better. They complimented rather than matched or mirrored you. With her in his life he would never be bored. Partnership was the willingness to not only follow but lead. To have someone who would lean on you as well as hold you up when you needed them to.

He wanted a lover, a friend, and a partner. Someone who tempted his body and challenged his mind. Diana was all those things.

He was a lucky fucker. Highdive brought his hand down in a slap across her ass. His cock throbbed as she gasped and arched up into his touch. The need to be inside her was so powerful it was as if she had put a spell on him.

He laughed. What had happened to the tightly controlled man who didn't believe any woman was worth taking a risk for? Diana was like no woman he'd ever known and that uniqueness was what had finally shown him that there were things other than Brotherhood worth fighting for.

She moaned as he brought his hand down on her ass a few more times. The flesh pinking under his blows was gorgeous. Unable to wait another second, he freed his cock barely pausing before thrusting into her depths. Her body welcomed his and he reveled in her tight warm embrace.

Gripping her hips with a ferocity he knew would leave bruises, Highdive let go of his control and set a brutal rhythm. It wasn't the time for long, gentle, love making. This was both a claiming and a celebration that together they had survived.

Time lost meaning as they came together. The world fading and coming into sharp definition as he took her. Their bodies were primed from the battle and needed this release more than they needed food or water.

Diana matched his frenzied pace with her own and he felt her tightening around him. Neither of them would last much longer. A growl ripped out of his throat as he used all of his strength to bring them together on every stroke.

The slap of their bodies meeting was a raw sound that pushed him faster. She screamed her pleasure, the sound a primal declaration. His orgasm slammed through him following hers. In that perfect moment it was as if they had connected on a soul deep level.

A high pitched buzzing broke them out of the spell that the intensity of their encounter had cast. Their stolen moment was coming to an end. Highdive shook his head as he pulled out of her. A small drone hovered above them.

"I think we've been caught." He gave Diana a light tap on her hip as he tucked himself back into his pants.

"I probably should have told them we were okay." She gave the flying camera a wave as she pulled up her pants.

There wasn't a single sign that she was at all embarrassed, or repentant for being caught fucking in the middle of combat. How perfect was she? Other than the sound of the drone there wasn't any other sound. The firefight at the Clubhouse must be over.

His chest tightened as he watched her finish pulling herself back together. She was like a perfect knife; graceful, beautiful, balanced, and deadly. A temptation to touch but you had to know how to handle her without getting hurt. His whole life he had never backed down from a challenge and he didn't intend to start now.

Highdive wrapped his arms around her and looked down into her golden-brown eyes. "I love you even if you are absolutely insane."

"Well I love you too." She took a deep breath. "I would follow you into Hell and drag you out if I had to. You need to understand there is nothing I wouldn't do to keep you safe."

"I think you stole my line." He brushed a gentle kiss across her lips.

"It's good we understand each other." Diana tossed her hair over her shoulder and looked up at the drone with a smile that made his heart stutter. "Do you think Cami will give us a copy of the video?"

Highdive threw back his head and laughed.

Epilogue

Not all girls are made of sugar, spice, and everything nice.
Some are made of sarcasm, wine, and everything fine.

W hy had she agreed to this? Diana had managed to go her whole life without wearing glitter in any form. Yet here she was in a black crop top with the words 'Property of a Dark Son' written across her chest in sparkly silver letters. It helped that her sister was with her wearing the same ridiculous top. She looked like she had never had more fun as she danced in the middle of the floor with the other identically dressed Old Ladies.

Going to Dark Secrets with friends was definitely different then her previous visits. Cami was the instigator of the evening but the clothing was courtesy of Val. The past month had been filled with the heartbreaking and exhausting tasks needed to recover from the attack on the compound. Diana couldn't argue that they all needed a break but sneaking away from the men to go to a sex club was a little more extreme than she would have planned.

"How long do you think it will take for the men to find us?" Tari asked.

They all knew it was a matter of when, not if. If it had been up to her she would have just told Highdive where she was going and probably arranged for him to meet her here later so they could relax and maybe get in some playtime. When she'd suggested it most of the women had scowled at her. Apparently the fun of 'girls night out' was to see if they could trick their men and then enjoy the punishments that would follow.

It amused her that most of the Old Ladies didn't realize that their men had hidden trackers in their Cuts and probably several other places. So it would have taken a lot more than ducking out of the back of a restaurant and driving off without their guard to avoid detection. Considering where they had ended up, Diana thought the point was more to force their men to come out and have fun as well.

The loss of their Brothers and the destruction of the Club-house had hit all of the Dark Sons hard. She understood having to focus when under pressure but if she had learned anything since being with Highdive it was that existing was not the same as living. Hopefully Pixie was right and this was exactly what was needed to remind them of that.

"Considering we're at a Dark Sons' business, I'm thinking we have about ten more minutes before they show up."

Especially since there were eight of them here. Pixie had pointed out that they needed to do something to shake off the gloom that was still hovering over everyone. Cami had come up with the cover story. Val created the wardrobe and her sister Alena had crafted the plan. Tari, Cat, Jade and Diana had agreed to tag along and now sat at the table while the other four danced like their lives depended on it.

"You think the staff will call them?" Jade looked horrified.

Diana and Cat laughed. It was still surprising how naive some of the women were about how sheltered and protected they were by their men.

"We didn't get two blocks from the restaurant without a tail." Diana nodded towards the door.

Jade turned around and gasped when she saw Decaf standing there with his arms crossed glaring at the dance floor. The man had been patched in last week, but still somehow ended up on babysitting duty. It was good to see his expression was more of exasperation rather than actual anger.

"How did he find us so quickly?" Jade asked.

The song ended and the dancers rushed over to the table taking long drinks from the waters they all had ordered earlier. It was still early in the evening so there weren't many people in the Club.

"This place is a hoot," Val said after she placed her drink down.

"I don't know, I was expecting more," Cami looked around, "w-Whips and chains."

"If you like those you should visit Jade's house," Alena teased.

Diana rolled her eyes, it was just like her sister to try and embarrass someone. "They are in the back or the private rooms. Most scenes don't start until after ten."

"Oh I want to see the p-private rooms!" Cami stood as if she was going to run off but Val tugged her back to the table.

"It is one thing to tweak your man's tail feathers. You go into the private rooms without Tek and you won't be getting a fun punishment."

"I gu-guess you're right." The purple-haired woman fidgeted. It was amazing how she never seemed to run out of energy. "So, Cat. You and M-Max going to be staying in Denver now?"

The Latina woman looked down and twirled her glass. "No. I love you guys but too many people here know me. I want a fresh start and Max is okay with that."

"You going back to Texas?" Val asked.

"Maybe. The Brothers there seemed like good people, but I'm not sure. We're going to do a cross-country ride and stay with different chapters. We'll decide where we're going to stay when we get tired of traveling."

The idea of moving around that much held no appeal to Diana as she'd done that most of her life. She was ready to settle in with Highdive. The previous week she'd even let people know that Tishina wasn't currently available for hire. Not that she was agreeing to never working as an assassin again; it would just be on a much more limited scale.

"Gives new meaning to riding off into the sunset." Tari smiled. "Very romantic."

"Bah! Her story isn't romantic, not when compared to mine and Hawk's! We were star-crossed lovers who had to spend years apart." Alena's Russian accent was on full display. Diana found the whole thing amusing.

"Have I ever told y'all how Dozer and I met? Now that is romantic."

The women spent the next ten minutes arguing over who had the best story. Diana didn't even try to compete. She knew hers was the best and didn't care what they thought. The Old Ladies were so distracted telling their tales that none of them noticed when the nine large men entered the Club.

While she was only interested in Highdive, she could admit that the wall of muscled flesh was impressive. Dressed all in black with their Cuts the only color they wore, the sheer dominance of the men was enough to cause everyone else in the Club to quiet down. Everyone appeared unable to look away as they stalked towards the table of arguing women.

Diana slipped away from the table leaving her new friends

to their fates. Highdive tracked her and they met in the shadow of one of the curtained play areas. His gaze raked over her and his lips tipped up in a smile as he took in her sparkly shirt.

"You didn't warn them?"

"I didn't want to spoil their fun. They went to a lot of trouble to distract their men and earn a punishment."

His hand wrapped around the back of her neck and she allowed herself to relax into his firm grip. It had been too long since she'd been able to fully give over to him like this.

"That was what they wanted, a distraction?" His grip tightened and her core clenched.

"Yes."

Highdive pulled her hair forcing her to stare up into his vibrant green eyes. "Is that how you answer my questions when we're here?"

The deep commanding tone in his voice sent chills across her skin. "No, Master."

"Then answer the question correctly. Did you want a distraction?"

"Yes, Master."

With those two words she let it all go. Handed over all her worries and concerns. Stopped thinking about where the exits were and where the closest weapons were located. No longer noticed how her friends were being taken away by their men for their own fun times. Her world focused down to the two of them standing face to face, his hand against her skin, their breaths mingling; they were so close.

Highdive's hand slid around her throat tracing the vein along her neck. Diana trembled as his finger tapped slowly to the beat of her heart. His lips brushed against hers.

"I think I can do that." He nipped her bottom lip. "Count for me."

1…2…3

Forever after never sounded so good.

Acknowledgments

We all have those days that kick us in the teeth and make it really hard to get back up. Well, 2022 hit me like a bad horror novel. Both my mind and body turned on me and I was unable to write or create anything. But unlike those scary tales that keep me from sleeping I was able to find light in my darkness in the form of family and friends. I'm slowly walking out into the sunshine because of your wonderful support.

I want to thank my family who stood by me during the darkest days and reminded me that every day has some success in it, as long as you keep trying. I love you.

To my best friend Mike who listened to me whine and kicked my ass when I needed it, Ride or Die babe!

Thank you to the wonderful staff at Blushing Books for being so understanding when this book should have been done months ago. Sandra, you are a goddess at editing! Patty, you are a jack-of-all-trades and amazing at all of them. And a special thanks to Bethany, who none of this would be possible without.

Finally, there is a special woman and fellow author who stepped up and kept things moving even when I couldn't. She is an Angel in disguise and deserves every ounce of good Karma the universe can send her. You are my sister from the other side of the continent. Thank you, Skyler West, with all my heart and soul.

Ann Jensen

I'm a snarky Jersey Woman who dreamed of one day becoming an Author. I write Romance with bigger than life characters who have to dodge every obstacle I gleefully throw in their paths. Somehow my characters also find time for steamy fun on their way to their HEAs.

I'm an avid reader, engineer, photographer, and a proud Bi woman. My life is a journey that I hope never stops in one place too long. I fill it with love and laughter whenever possible and when I can't, I pull out my clue by four and use it with deadly precision.

https://annjensenwrites.com/

Dark Sons Motorcycle Club
Saved by the Dark
Lost in the Dark
Caught in the Dark
Undercover In the Dark
Leap Into the Dark
Bound in the Dark

Blushing Books

Blushing Books is the oldest eBook publisher on the web. We've been running websites that publish steamy romance and erotica since 1999, and we have been selling eBooks since 2003. We have free and promotional offerings that change weekly, so please do visit us at http://www.blushingbooks.com/free.

Blushing Books Newsletter

Please join the Blushing Books newsletter
to receive updates & special promotional offers.
You can also join by using your mobile phone:
Just text BLUSHING to 22828.

Every month, one new sign up via text messaging will receive
a $25.00 Amazon gift card, so sign up today!